ELUSIVE GETAWAY

ELUSIVE GETAWAY

— A Novel —

RONALD LUTZ

LUMINARE PRESS

WWW.LUMINAREPRESS.COM

Elusive Getaway
Copyright © 2020 by Ronald Lutz

Printed in the United States of America

Cover Design by Melissa K. Thomas

Luminare Press
442 Charnelton St.
Eugene, OR 97401
www.luminarepress.com

LCCN: 2019920581
ISBN: 978-1-64388-278-9

Proverbs 14:10—Each heart knows its own
bitterness, and no one else can share its joy.

Introduction

— October 1 —

A HANDSOME FLOOR-STANDING WORLD GLOBE AND AN OVERSIZE sofa were conspicuous furnishings in the den in the home of James Wilson, the leader of the Australian Senate. The room was trimmed in dark walnut and lit by recessed lighting and also had several other armchairs, end tables, and reading lamps; three walls were lined with bookcases filled with law books and literary works. Two men, Wilson and Prime Minister Johnathan Barnes, came into the room wearing tailored suits and holding whiskey tumbler glasses filled half full with bourbon. Wilson, smoking a cigarette, listened to the prime minister.

A hidden video/audio device recorded their conversation.

"...(unintelligible) and Brown has some good early numbers." He's polling well," said Barnes.

"Probably because he's hired Dowling," offered Wilson. "Those numbers will change. It won't interrupt any of our arrangements if that's what you're thinking."

"But I heard you suspended the boat traffic."

"Only Sea Charter," he said, taking a drag on his cigarette. "I put them on hold until we find a new pilot. The guy hired for the Brisbane run filed a report on the illegal immigrants."

"Home Affairs tracks those reports," Barnes grumbled.

"Not this one; it was shredded," said Wilson. "I have that paper-work screened. But the men he transported were lost."

"Who filed the report?" Barnes asked.

"Denham, Mike Denham. And he couldn't repay what he cost us in his lifetime, which won't last much longer," Wilson stated. "When the time is right, I'll deal with him."

"I've heard rumors about what happens to someone who gets in your way. Just don't jeopardize your standing with the public," Barnes advised. "You can't afford to have adverse publicity this close to elections. Why not rally the base—make an announcement you've got votes for immigration reform?"

"What for? You'd just recommend another veto."

Barnes smiled. "Yes. But I'd be the bad guy, not you." He sipped his drink. "What's going on with our Iranian deal?"

"I put talks on hold till after the elections. There's no hurry. It may boost our price this way," he said. "And as long as we keep our talks under wraps, our money train stays right on track. We have to avoid publicity on this too. If the media find out, or those guys in Foreign Affairs, it's a deal-breaker."

"I know, Jim. Like you say, there's no hurry," Barnes said, and then took another drink. Pondering his glass he went on, "I've been told you're still bribing some of our contractors."

"Where'd you hear that?" Wilson asked, visibly unhappy.

"I'm not going to say; you'll go off half-cocked. But if they start shouting kickback ...well, your boat operator filing a report with immigration will seem like small potatoes."

"I've never had any problems with the contractors and don't expect to." He took another long drag on his cigarette.

Barnes said, "But you could have a political problem. Your poll numbers are weak in two demographics: Africans and women. You'll be okay this election, but it's a concern."

"Then I'll worry about it later," Wilson stated.

"Times are changing, Jim. The right woman could boost your women vote, just ask my wife," Barnes said, smiling again.

"The so-called ladies I see now aren't exactly what you would call the get-out-to-vote type. I'll tell you what I'm not going to do, date a black woman like my son."

                    Ronald Lutz

"A black woman?" Barnes probed, "I've heard they can be uninhibited, if you know what I mean. Have you met her?"

"Of course not. It's been years since I've even talked with my son. But I'm getting to know her with EDI."

"EDI?"

"Electronic Data Interchange. The program I told you to support. We passed it on your recommendation, remember?"

"Can't say I do."

"It's like WikiLeaks—getting personal info from private networks. Like from my son's dating friend. With EDI I can check on her and make sure their relationship won't be trouble for my campaign. Sometimes I think my son is with her to spite me. He knows how I feel about interracial couples."

"Use it to your advantage, Jim," Barnes said. "Show them you're tolerant. It will play as a positive. You'll see I'm right on this one. As for me, I think I'll take a look at EDI."

"It's set up in my office. I'll show you how it works."

CHAPTER ONE

— October 2 —

Harriet White was an eye-catching twenty-three-year-old African American woman standing five feet, eight inches tall without shoes and wearing a gray cotton tunic, print leggings, and black loafers; her tousled hair was cut short. An international student from Sacramento, California in the United States, she was in her second year of graduate school at the University of Sydney in Australia with a dual major in the fields of social and political science. As a volunteer for the campaign of Leonard Brown, opposing the reelection of James Wilson for the New South Wales Senate seat, her contribution was distributing fliers in the Sydney suburbs. She signed on to the Brown campaign thinking it might be a good opportunity to work on her thesis, "Gerrymandering: Its Political Impact in the State of New South Wales." But an even more compelling reason was that her boyfriend, Scott Wilson, also worked as a volunteer for Brown. It was a way to stay close to him. Conversely, in the last five years she had visited her parents only twice. They saw her one other time while taking an Australian tour.

Entering the Brown headquarters annex to get more fliers, she was stopped by technical consultant Terry Godfrey and his partner, Shepherd Raburn. The men, in their mid-twenties, were Caucasian and similarly dressed, wearing Levi's jeans and T-shirts with an imprint that read "think geek." She was asked to look at the video that had been recorded in the Wilson den. Harriet accompanied Terry to a workstation and sat down to watch as "Shep" played the videotape on a laptop computer. After it was over, they waited for her reaction. She was speechless.

"No need for captions," Terry said. "It speaks for itself. We can distribute it to the media like it is if Leonard gives the go-ahead."

"I can't believe they talked about me," she said unhappily. "At least they didn't mention my name."

"We would have edited it out," Shep said. "But we thought you should see it just the same."

"How'd you get it?" she questioned.

"Fiber technology and a little grunt work," Terry stated. "Shep installed a camera and recorder in Wilson's home."

"Was that legal?" she asked, knowing that it was not.

"No," Terry remarked, "but in this case we felt the end justified the means."

"Scott knew the layout," Shep offered, "and after he got the repair order for new track lights it was easy."

"He gets back tomorrow," she said. "I'll tell him what you've got ...unless, can you make a copy. I could show it to him when he gets home. It would have to be on a DVD."

"Why not?" Terry handed Shep a blank DVD. "But I'll tell Ray so he'll know what we did."

"He's become a paranoid control freak," said Shep.

"Well, I can understand that," Terry stated. "Using fiber optics has us all on edge."

"This nails Wilson," Shep said. "It gets Barnes too. Just what Ray hoped for."

Shep gave her a copy of the recording in a paper sleeve when it was finished.

———

THE NEXT DAY HARRIET DROVE TO THE AIRPORT TO PICK UP Scott, who was returning from a two-week assignment with CARE in Jakarta, Indonesia. They had not been together in over two weeks, the longest they had been apart since they met two years earlier.

They both had attended an Ultimate Business Support conference. She was required to go to fulfill a college course requirement for a study group. He was asked to go as a condition of employment by CARE. Scott had completed his studies at the University of Newcastle with a bachelor of arts degree, and his position with CARE was guaranteed pending completion of the seminar. When he sat next to her, they hit it off almost immediately and began dating regularly. Because they had become close, she decided not to return to America after completing her studies. It was a decision she knew would greatly disappoint her parents.

As his 2:00 p.m. Qantas flight was taxiing to the arrival gate her excitement at seeing him increased. They had talked on the phone every day while he was in Jakarta. She wanted to call him as his plane approached the gate but realized in her eagerness to see him she had left her phone in the car. Inside the airbus, the passengers prepared to disembark. Scott stood up and grabbed his brown carry-on bag—it was embossed with the letters SW—and waited for people in front of him to begin to exit.

Caucasian and twenty-four years old, he was six feet, three inches tall with brown hair and wore contact lenses. Dressed in a pale green Henley shirt, khaki pants, and boat shoes with no socks, he was also looking forward to their reunion.

While waiting to exit the plane he tried to phone Harriet, but there was no answer. Suddenly it occurred to him that he hadn't called his mother since leaving, even though Harriet reminded him several times. He made his way to baggage claim and then pretended not to notice her creeping up behind him. Dressed all in white—shorts, top, and tennis shoes—she gently touched his shoulder. He turned and pulled her to him. They hugged and kissed passionately, causing some other travelers to react uneasily. Still in an embrace, Harriet saw his "SW" bag on the carousel and leaned back from his grasp to point to the suitcase. Scott pulled it off the belt, and she picked up his carry-on. They walked together into the main terminal.

"Did you see any attractive women in Jakarta?" she asked.

"They were everywhere," he replied, "but none as beautiful as you."

"Liar," she responded, smiling broadly.

"It's true," he proclaimed. "In fact, in all the places I've been, I can think of only one woman who may be more beautiful than you."

Harriet continued to smile: "Your mother."

"How 'bout we go see her. You know, I didn't call her once while I was away."

"I'm sure you'll be forgiven," she said. "The car's in P2."

Scott drove her lime green, four-door Kia Rio to his mother's home at her Balmoral estate.

<hr>

Harriet rented a house on a corner lot at the entrance of a cul-de-sac on Pine Street in Marrickville. It was a large ranch-style home with a deck and garage. Coming from the Balmoral estate and the visit with his mother, Scott parked her Kia Rio at the front curb, where he often parked his own car. They entered the home kissing and pawing at one another in a hurry to get in bed.

"Where's your housemate?" he asked breathlessly.

"I forgot to tell you," she answered, continuing to smother him with kisses. "She took the job in Canberra. She moved out day before yesterday."

"I knew I'd find a reason to like her," he declared.

He dropped his suitcase, but she carried his briefcase into the bedroom and blindly tossed it so the bag came to rest right-side up at the foot of the bed. In no time at all, they had engaged in a sexual union two times over. Their two weeks apart led to intensely passionate lovemaking that ended with both of them happy, satisfied, and exhausted.

As they snuggled together, she examined his face with probing brown eyes before turning aside to put on a music CD and then light a cigarette. He forced a tolerant expression.

"What? It's my first one in over a month," she explained.

"I didn't say anything."

"You were thinking it," she said, gently poking him.

Scott smiled happily, and then pulled her close to him. "I think we need some wine," he said in a seductive voice and released his hold on her to get out of bed.

"Don't be too long," she murmured.

While he was in the kitchen, she slipped into her bathrobe and removed the CD from the stereo, placing it on the edge of the bed in a paper sleeve. Scott returned, and they enjoyed a glass of wine. He noticed his briefcase at the foot of the bed and, opening it, took out a ring box and gave it to her.

"What's this!" she exclaimed. "You didn't!"

He put the ring on her finger. She inspected it closely and then showered him with kisses before looking at it again.

"It's beautiful! I adore it."

"The guy at the pawnshop said you would," he teased.

"Yooou!" Then she broke into a smile.

"I love you, Harriet. Will you marry me?"

"Yes! I love you."

They kissed and held a long embrace.

She pulled back from the hug. "What about my parents?"

"They know about us," he declared.

"But they're wanting me to return to California."

"We can do that," he offered.

"We?"

"They'll want to meet me, and I should meet them."

She smiled. "That's a long way. What about your job?"

"We can work it out," he said and kissed her on the cheek.

"Okay, if you say so," she said without hesitation, then added, "Can we change the subject?"

"Okay. Yours or mine?"

"Me first," she said. "I think your father knows about us."

"Well, surprise, surprise ...What makes you say that?"

"A guy stopped me in the mall and handed me a Wilson campaign button," she continued, while pushing hair off his forehead with her hand. "He said be careful who you run around with and then walked away. I mean, it was a bit unnerving. It felt very much like a threat."

"Was he someone you've seen before?"

"No. Maybe he thought I was somebody else?"

"Yeah, we should be so lucky."

"There's something else." She pulled the DVD from her robe pocket and handed it to him in its paper sleeve. "Terry made it for me yesterday. It's a copy of a videotape from the equipment set up in your father's home. They're ready to distribute it to the media if Mr. Brown gives the okay."

"Good ole Terry," Scott chortled. "What's he got?"

Scott's face was beaming as he moved to the DVD player.

They both were mesmerized as they watched the recording.

When the video ended, Harriet removed the DVD, put it back in the paper sleeve, and placed it on the bed next to the CD.

"Can you believe we got that?" Scott said.

"And that I'm being hacked," Harriet added. "Is your father a racist?"

"Yes. From the old school," Scott replied.

"How many other private networks do you suppose he's looking at?"

"I don't know, but when the video goes public I'll bet he won't be searching networks anymore" Scott suggested, "or using data collection."

"And the other things," she added. "It's as if they're running a syndicate: kickbacks, Indonesians, Iranian deals."

"Every time they open their mouths they incriminate themselves," he said. "I don't think Mr. Brown will have any trouble okaying this one."

A gunmetal gray Hyundai Elantra drove onto Pine Street, marked as a "no exit road," and continued on past several houses to the cul-de-sac. Rounding the loop at the end of the court, the car retraced its path before stopping across the street from the Kia Rio parked in front of the brick ranch-style house. The house was landscaped along the front foundation with shrubbery and carpet roses. The lawn was manicured, and patches of short ornamental grass bordered the walk to the door; a side deck wrapped around to the back of the house and was hidden by a hedgerow. Several Eucalyptus trees provided shade. The driver of the Elantra checked the house address and then pulled a vehicle registry list from his coat pocket to verify the owner of the Rio. The neighborhood was quiet; the evening dusk had settled.

The man in the car was in his late thirties with thick, curly black hair and appeared to be fit and trim. He wore a black pin-striped suit, white shirt, and navy blue tie. His chiseled face was expressionless, and he could have been considered handsome except for a long scar that ran from high on his left cheekbone to near the corner of his lip.

Removing his seatbelt, he placed a call to the Sydney Harbour Marriott Hotel on Circular Quay where a Wilson campaign rally was already underway. A capacity crowd of two hundred and fifty people were celebrating, and all seemed to be in a jovial, boisterous mood. Compared to a Brown campaign dinner of several couples, this was an extravaganza.

No doubt the frame of mind of the crowd was fortified by the temporary open bar, even though it was subsidized by a one-hundred-dollar liquor fee charged to each person when they came into the room; no one could have entered the event by mistake. The walls were splashed with posters and pictures of the candidate. Numerous banners hung from the ceiling, and throughout the room a number of slogans were displayed, including one that read "I'll Fight Corruption."

Campaign manager Francis Offerman stood at a lectern at the other end of the room from the bar and announced better than expected recent poll numbers. The crowd cheered louder, followed by a chant of "speech, speech," reaching a crescendo and crying out for Wilson to speak. He was seated next to the lectern, impeccably dressed in a blue suit with a gray tie. Wilson was reveling along with everyone until he paused to answer a call. The crowd noise lessened when he held his phone high and then to his ear to indicate he was engaged for the moment.

"Looks like she's in the house," said the man in the car.

"Okay. We've taken care of the annex," Wilson told him. "All that's left is for you to find the girl's DVD and bust it up. My son may be there, but don't let him or anyone else stop you. Smash it up!"

Just then a silver Nissan Sentra stopped behind the Rio. Dark tinted windows prevented the man in the Elantra from being seen, but even in near-dark he saw the Sentra driver.

"Dowling just drove up," he said to Wilson.

"You sure?"

"No mistakin' that guy."

"Is he going to the house?" Wilson asked.

"He's still in the car. It looks like he's checking the address on the GPS readout."

"That SOB. He's there for the video. Don't let him get in your way. In fact...you got a gun?" Wilson asked.

"Yeah," the man in the car responded.

"Okay, let's take care of Mr. Dowling once and for all." Wilson paused, "In fact, let's make it two for one."

"Two?" the man questioned.

"If he goes inside and the girl's there, pop him and then pop the girl like he killed her then shot himself."

"I can do that," the man in the car said without emotion.

"If anyone else is there, use your own judgment," Wilson said. "But bust up the DVD, and if my son's there, bring him to the house so the media won't know he was there."

"He's out of the car," the man said, ending the call.

When Wilson put down his phone, cries for him to speak rang out again. Stepping to the podium, he pronounced a few insolent remarks about his opponent and ended an abbreviated speech

 Ronald Lutz

with rallying cries. Then balloons suspended from nets attached to the ceiling were released along with paper confetti marking an end to the festivities. His speech had been short because he wanted to return home to finalize a plan that would prevent his son from being linked to what was happening that night. He knew if Scott was implicated, he would be too.

The man in the car put on latex gloves, then removed a handgun from a valise on the passenger seat and attached a silencer. Getting out of the car, he crossed the street and crouched down a few yards behind Dowling, who was at the front door. Inside the house, in the bedroom, Harriet was watching Scott dress. They agreed he could use her car to get his mail that had accumulated in his rental box while he was away, but he was to hurry back. He would stay the night, and she would drive him to his apartment the next day. After all, they were engaged; they would not spend the night apart.

They were in an embrace when the doorbell rang. Harriet flinched and looked at Scott with surprise. The chime rang again. Cinching her robe, she walked to the door with Scott right behind her. The bell rang a third time. Through the peephole she saw Ray Dowling. When she opened the door, he charged inside and the gunman crept to the open door to try and see who else was in the room.

"Where's the DVD you got from Terry?" Ray demanded.

"What's going on?" Scott asked. "Isn't it a ...?"

Ray floored him with a sucker punch; his head hit a corner of the desk as he fell, knocking him out. Harriet screamed. The man at the door glanced inside as she knelt down over Scott. Seeing he was unconscious, she looked up at Ray.

"What are you doing?" she yelled at him.

"The smug bloody knob; he's like his daddy, gettin' in the way where he ain't wanted."

"What are you talking about?" she moaned.

"I want the DVD Terry gave you, for Christ's sake."

"It's a copy of the one at the annex," she said, holding back tears. "Why bother us? Why bother Scott? He didn't know about it until a few minutes ago."

"I worked years for his ole man and never said a thing; the DVD exposes him for who he is. Where is it?" he demanded.

"That's no reason to hit Scott," she cried.

"You're wasting time," he advised. "He'll be alright. I need to get the DVD to the media before his old man finds out. Now, where is it?"

"In the bedroom," she answered sadly, still at Scott's side.

"Get it!"

She got up and paused to switch on a ceiling fan and open a deck door, hoping the air would help revive Scott. Pushing her along, they moved toward the bedroom while the gunman stepped quietly into the house and scanned the dimly lit interior. The floor had gold wall-to-wall carpet. A bookcase divided the large room. One side had furniture in a semicircle facing a television; the other side of the room had a couch, matching chair, the desk, artificial plants, and a fireplace inserted in the end wall. French doors opened onto the deck. Scott was lying on the floor next to the desk.

Harriet and Ray walked into a hallway. She immediately turned into her bedroom and went to the bed. He watched her from the hall entrance, blocking the view of the gunman. She picked up the DVD and extended her arm with it in her hand toward Ray. Just as he started to reach for it Scott groaned. Startled, Ray turned and looked at him. In the dim light his peripheral vision did not extend enough for him to see the man behind him near the wall. Scott moaned again but remained unconscious as Ray watched.

When Ray turned back he said, "He'll be all right. I'll..."

A gunshot to the side of his head cut his sentence short; he was dead before he hit the floor. Stunned, Harriet was unable to move. The gunman stepped forward and reached out with his other gloved hand.

"I'll take that," he said, referring to the disc in her hand.

     Ronald Lutz

At his words, she shifted slightly, and the disc slid from her fingers to the floor. She looked at him with a fatalistic gaze as a bullet pierced her heart. Removing the silencer, he pressed the gun into the hand of Dowling, then picked up the disc that Harriet had dropped to the floor and broke it into pieces.

Scott remained unconscious as the gunman began to look for something to tie him up. After a short time, he woke up and saw Ray on the floor and began crawling toward him. Then he noticed the lifeless body of Harriet and, standing up, moved toward her, but the gunman intervened. He used a cord of rope he found in a kitchen drawer and forced Scott to sit in a chair, tying his arms and legs, and put a handkerchief in his mouth as a gag.

"Did you do this?" Scott mumbled through the gag.

"You got more bags," he asked. "We've got to go. Your old man doesn't want any publicity from you being here."

Scott, slightly more coherent, said, "My father hired you to do this?"

"She had a DVD she wasn't supposed to have. All the others were torched at the annex," he replied. "Too bad for her Dowling had to show up."

Still talking through the gag, Scott yelled out, "You son-of-a-bitch! You did this because of a DVD?"

The gunman went through the rest of the house looking for anything that belonged to Scott. Checking in the bedroom, he saw the carry-on bag with the SW embossment and carried it into the living room, setting it next to Scott's suitcase.

"Is this all?" he asked, then demanded, "Let's go!"

The man untied Scott's legs. He picked up the bags with one arm and pushed Scott out the door. In the car, the gunman removed the handkerchief from his mouth at which point Scott asked him if he could call for an ambulance. To his surprise, the man said okay.

CHAPTER TWO

One week before Harriet and Ray were murdered a more subtle form of interpersonal tension was about to play out in the home of Jennifer and Mike Denham. While she breathed softly, asleep on the bed next to her husband, he observed her dispassionately, awake because of what he had read on their computer. He seldom went near it. But the previous evening Jennifer, sitting at the desk looking at the monitor, answered a cell phone call and walked outside to get a better reception. It was then, while searching in the desk for ship documents required for his voyage the next day, he paused to read her letter "To David" on the screen. He could have been embarrassed, she wrote with such frankness and passion. She often failed to close her email folder. He had mentioned it to her one time, but she said it wasn't an issue; there was nothing to hide.

The display on the digital clock jumped to 5:00 a.m. He rolled gently out of bed, and putting the thought of the email aside, he was able to consider the ocean voyage later that day on the converted ferry *Aurora*. His employer, Sea Charter Tours, was offering him triple pay plus a bonus to command the ship and test its ability on the sea, but for him the money was secondary to being on the ocean again.

He had already steered the ferry on short runs with no cargo, once from Sydney Harbour to Shell Harbour in the south, and a second time to Newcastle in the north; both times she handled the sea at an even keel. Now he was being asked to take the ship round trip from Sydney to Brisbane, running her with no cargo outbound but transporting a full load on the return trip to Sydney. He expected no problems.

There was plenty of time to shave and bathe, and when he finished his shower he stopped to examine himself in the full-length mirror. About six feet tall, with brown hair and brown eyes, his forty-three-year-old body looked to be in good shape. Jennifer, now awake and standing in the bedroom darkness, made her own examination, inspecting him from head to toe.

"You know," she said, walking into the doorway, "you're still pretty fit and trim considering your age." He turned to face her, and she noticed the semblance of a smile at the corner of his mouth. She continued, "But you can't deny it's the female body that's a thing of beauty. The male ...it's serviceable at best."

"What about David?" he asked, as he toweled himself dry.

As they made eye contact her calm facial expression had turned to puzzlement.

"Michelangelo's David," he put forward.

She blinked and coaxed a smile. "Well, there are a few exceptions, I suppose."

The corner of his mouth turned up again, this time more of a smirk than a smile. He put down the towel, walked into the bedroom, and began to dress.

"You're taking another ship out?" she asked. "For how long? I was tired last night; I can't remember what you said."

"Four or five days. Takin' a ship to Brisbane and back."

"It's some kind of tryout?"

"Yeah, a test run."

He finished dressing and stood up; they looked at one another again for a moment and, not able to think of anything else to say, she began to loosen her gown.

"Well, now that I'm up I may as well take a shower too," she said, removing her lingerie and exposing a most attractive, fit and trim body to him. Showing him a tight-lipped smile, she gave a seductive nod.

"Better make it a cold one," he said. "I've gotta go."

"You're no fun," she said, exhaling as he left the room.

———

AS THE SUN NEARED THE FAR HORIZON THAT EVENING, ITS RAYS reflected off the waters of Middle Harbour and could be seen at a house on Pitt Street in the exclusive Balmoral neighborhood of Sydney. The home was a mansion and had a living space of twelve-thousand, six-hundred square feet; it was the central feature of a sixty-acre walled estate that included an Olympic-sized pool, an attached conservatory and a three-bay car garage; the lavish gardens were well maintained with trimmed hedges and decorative fountains. Nine full-time and ten part-time personnel were employed at the estate, including a chauffeur, four groundskeepers, a pool maintenance woman, and ten staff in the home. Henry and Henrietta, two house-trained Scottish Terriers, often roamed the grounds.

The sunset dispersed a soft twilight glow as visitors drove into the estate and followed a brick-paved road that curved through a line of trees, stopping under a portico at the entrance to the home. There, they were greeted by the owner, Margaret Farrow, sitting in her motorized wheelchair.

Eleven years earlier she had been paralyzed on her left side after falling down a flight of stairs, but by working with physical and occupational therapists each week in a moderate exercise regimen, the fifty-three-year-old woman was able to maintain a level of fitness and keep a positive outlook.

Three personal aides helped her follow an ambitious schedule that outpaced many of her contemporaries. She was president of the county historical society, advocate for metro libraries, and a respected board member of several firms headquartered in Sydney. No one could say she did not try to keep busy. And like her mother, she was interested in clothing fabrication and design. To greet the guests, she decided to wear a light gray flower print dress from Eric;

 Ronald Lutz

her brown hair was cut elegantly short. Invigorated by the warm early spring day, she chose to sit outside. All the visitors remarked favorably about her dress and, inside the home, enjoyed drinks and an appetizer. As she waited for one last car to approach the house, her thoughts were increasingly on her son, Scott, who was in Indonesia on an assignment with CARE Australia, his first overseas trip.

Ray Dowling, one of the guests and a longtime friend, came outside and sat next to her on the balustrade railing. She smiled at him but said nothing. Silence was not typical of their relationship, and recognizing her frame of mind, he smiled and waited with her as she watched for the last expected guest. They both attended Macquarie University thirty years earlier. Remaining close ever since that time, they freely and easily exchanged points of view without a sense of self-importance or embarrassment, but Ray had become slovenly in his fifties and being overweight and balding contributed to his unkempt look. He had a craggy face and pointed chin and had shaved a scruffy beard before coming to the dinner.

Ray was the campaign communication specialist for New South Wales Governor Leonard Brown, Senate candidate for the Liberal party. Brown was in the last car to arrive, along with his wife Carol and campaign manager Grace Ackerman. Four other couples invited for dinner were there to screen new television advertisements created for the Brown candidacy. The four couples and Margaret were key Brown contributors, giving him eighty percent of his private money.

Prior to viewing the new ads, Margaret had a five-course meal served featuring leg of lamb. The twelve diners paired up at the table: Dr. Tompkins and his wife Edith, David and Naomi Walters, Thomas and Lois Nettleton, and Jonathan and Caroline Busby all sat beside partners other than their spouse. Following the meal, they were asked to assemble in the home theater to view the advertisements. Everyone began to move deliberately from their seats at the table and several took the opportunity to use the washroom. Grace paused at the floor to ceiling windows that overlooked the harbor to enjoy the twinkling lights and joined the Nettletons who were also admiring the nighttime sights of Middle Harbour.

"It's a nice view," said Mr. Nettleton, "but if it faced west you could watch the sunset."

"Or get up and watch the sunrise," Grace chuckled as she added, "then go back to bed."

"I've got the same view on Long Bay," said David Walters, walking up to the window, "if I climb on my roof."

"What are we going to be watching?" Dr. Tompkins asked as he stopped to inquire of Grace.

"We've got some new television ads," Grace answered. "You'll be able to see how we're spending your money."

"I hope they're better than what you've got now," said Mr. Nettleton. "The ones I've seen don't do much for me."

"Ray hired a new production staff. I think you'll see a big difference," she said.

"And we think the new ads will help solidify our public funding," said Gov. Brown, joining the group.

"You know better than me," said Mr. Nettleton. "You'll hang on to that funding by keeping your poll numbers up."

"Our staff is planning a greater nationwide promotion for just that reason. And we've negotiated different time slots for the ads. They'll be shown on all major channels," Brown said.

Leonard Brown, challenging the longtime incumbent James Wilson, had been governor for six years in what was viewed as mostly a ceremonial post, but he earned the respect of state lawmakers by being a dispute moderator and a tough negotiator while helping to enact legislation. Prior to his term as governor, he served six years on the New South Wales Legislative Council.

Before entering politics, Brown owned profitable vineyards in southern New South Wales that grew Chardonnay grapes. He and his wife, formerly Carol Newley, the daughter of another successful vineyard operator, had been married for twenty-five years and had raised three children.

"A nationwide promotion won't work if you don't have a better strategy. If you ask me, different ad placement isn't going to help much," Mr. Nettleton said skeptically.

"I want to give them a chance," said the governor. "I think these new ones will be a big improvement."

Mr. Nettleton was not convinced, shaking his head negatively.

"If you'll join us, the others are waiting," Margaret said, approaching in her wheelchair and guiding them to the theater.

Grace had put together eight advertisements, produced by Ray and his staff, for an initial viewing. Ready to premiere as early as the next day, the advertisements depicted the governor with a more positive message. The presentation took about forty minutes. When it was over most everyone liked what they had seen. The governor then made another plea for additional money.

"We've had a busy campaign the first couple of weeks and the early polls are encouraging," he said. "We've kept our public funding because of those polls, but the next eight weeks before elections we'll need more money to pay our new staff and to pay for travel and advertising to support our nationwide effort."

"You're sure this is the right way to go?" asked Jonathan Busby, seated next to his wife. "I rather liked some of the attack ads. It was time someone started showing Wilson in a negative light."

"I like the ones we've just seen," said Mrs. Tompkins. "I get so tired of seeing negative ones all the time."

"I couldn't agree more," said Mrs. Nettleton.

"I asked Ray and his staff to put these together," added Gov. Brown. "They've done a great job. Of course, better quality translates to higher cost."

"And that's what you want us to pay," stated Mr. Busby. "How soon will you need the money?"

"If there was only some way we could know they'd be worth our investment," stated Mr. Walters.

"Well, if the ads start tomorrow," added Mrs. Busby, "we should see some poll movement."

"Can we wait a while and see what the reaction is?" Dr. Tompkins asked.

"The networks want the money upfront," answered Gov. Brown. "Our public funds will cover that for the time being."

"I don't think we'll need to rely solely on these ads to dictate a way forward," Ray interjected.

"But that's all we've got, isn't it?" said Mrs. Busby

"Maybe not," answered Ray.

Brown hired Ray as a technical supervisor, but his overall campaign experience was unmatched. In politics thirty-two years after graduating from college with a communication and media major, he first volunteered for a job in Africa before working twenty years for Brown's opponent, James Wilson.

"Why not debate Wilson?" inquired Mr. Nettleton.

"His campaign always puts us off," replied the governor.

"It looks like we all need more time to think about it," Margaret offered. "Why don't we meet here again in two weeks and try to decide. And I'll plan another dinner."

Margaret, like Ray, had also been a former Labor Party supporter. She was married to James Wilson for over nineteen years. They shared a son, Scott. Her support and marriage ended ten years ago, not long after her fall. While Margaret was being praised for the meal, Ray approached Gov. Brown.

"The new ads are good," Ray offered, "but we're close to getting something even better. Something that might expose Wilson's conduct since he's been in office. It could change the course of our campaign."

"I understand, Ray," said Gov. Brown. "I'm eager to see what you've got. Let's just not get ahead of ourselves."

"Okay, but it may turn out to be a big deal," Ray promised.

CHAPTER THREE

Jennifer had been a year junior to Mike in high school. They met at a dance and had a brief teenage affair, but his decision to leave school and join the navy ended their courtship. Both were on separate paths. Her goal was to become a journalist, and four years of study in college led to a career at a local newspaper. After the navy, he worked his way to the captaincy of a superyacht. They remained single, intent on their chosen occupations.

A dozen years after high school they met again; he fell in love with her, and she loved being loved. Marriage followed and so did contentment for a while; they were in their early thirties and planned to have children, but she was kept busy working on the paper, and Mike was often away on the yacht. Her inability to conceive during this time was frustrating for them both. A test showed he was fertile. However, her exam revealed one fallopian tube was blocked, so fertility treatments were prescribed in hopes of assisting pregnancy. That was when she asked him to get a job closer to home, thinking it would give them more opportunities for her to conceive.

He found work on a local cruise ship. But when it began to sail to more distant ports, she again tried to persuade him to change positions and find something that would keep him in Sydney. Bothered by her request—it seemed she was asking him to choose between her and the sea—he decided to sign on for another year with the cruise line, essentially walking out on their marriage of five years. It reminded her of when he left high school to join the navy.

They were apart for a year but when it came time to sign an agreement for a third-year cruise, he rejected the contract. He missed Jennifer and hoped to reconnect with her by taking a position working on a charter boat for Emerald Tours in Sydney Harbour. During their separation her work and private life had become a mess. It didn't improve when she had an affair. Instead of a satisfying tryst, the relationship caused her even more misery. When she learned Mike was working on the charter boat, she signed up to be a passenger on one of his tours. She was eager for a reconciliation, too. The meeting eventually led to a mutual understanding and the realization that more work was needed to solidify their marriage.

There was no need to renew their vows, but they decided their marriage had to be a priority. When they were ready to start a family, and it wasn't possible by the natural method, they could explore other ways, including adoption. Their first five years were a roller-coaster ride, bottoming out when they separated. When they reunited, it was more like friendly bumper cars. On their tenth wedding anniversary there was no celebration, and only a few days later Mike came across the email.

THE *AURORA* TRIAL RUN MIKE PILOTED WAS UNEVENTFUL UNTIL he reached Brisbane. There, two hundred immigrant laborers boarded for the return trip to Sydney, the promised full cargo load. Mike was certain they were illegal Indonesian workers, but the Brisbane harbor master informed him city officials had cleared the voyage. Unable to contact the office of Sea Charter, his only other option was to take the men to Sydney and inform immigration. He called the Sydney harbor master and told him to expect his arrival with a cargo of illegal aliens.

On the return trip, he received a dispatch communication instructing him to harbor at Gosford, north of Sydney. A follow-up message confirmed he was to anchor near the town. Once in the

     Ronald Lutz

harbor, the men being transported jumped ship and escaped into the adjacent countryside. On the fourth day after his departure date, Mike returned to Sydney and filed a report with the Office of Immigration. He was told it would be processed as an action review and returned to Sea Charter only to learn his report had been dismissed and the review ignored. He also discovered his pay for the *Aurora* trip was being withheld because of contractual violations having to do with the loss of cargo, and he was discharged with no other explanation.

CHAPTER FOUR

— October 3 —

Earlier on the day of the murders, Scott and Harriet had arrived at his mother's Balmoral estate from the airport and entering the house were greeted by Henry and Henrietta and Sandra Morse, one of Margaret's personal attendants. Sandra was wearing a leisure suit accessorized with gardening gloves, pruning shears, and an enamel watering can and walked with them as far as the flower beds near the patio. Margaret was there in her wheelchair under a table umbrella reviewing some financial reports, one of her responsibilities as a member of a corporate board. She was dressed in a gray business suit, having returned from a corporate meeting earlier in the day. Sandra walked to the edge of the patio and tried to give full attention to watering the plants while listening in on their conversation.

"Hello mother," Scott met her with a kiss. "How are you?"

"I thought you had abandoned me," she teased.

"You know better than that; I told you I was going to Jakarta."

"And was that too far away for you to use the phone in your pocket to call and say hello," she continued. "But that's alright. You're here now so you can tell me all about Jakarta and your conference. How are you, Harriet?"

"Fine. You look wonderful. And you've cut your hair."

"The ladies at the Lyceum Club encouraged me to do it."

"A short bob suits you," Harriet said. "I like it."

They were seated by now and Scott inquired about her health again and, when satisfied all was well, began to talk about his time in Indonesia. Harriet was content to sit back and listen. After a bit, Margaret called the kitchen and asked them to serve refreshments; lemonade, cheese, and crackers were soon on the table. The three continued to visit for over an hour until Scott excused himself to use the washroom. Sandra took a break from gardening to clear the table while Margaret and Harriet continued to talk.

"I appreciated your calls while Scott was gone," Margaret said. "But I never asked about you. Have you been busy?"

"I worked quite a lot on my thesis; I'm almost finished."

"You told me once what it's about, but I forget."

"Gerrymandering's political impact in New South Wales."

"I'd like to read it when you're through," Margaret stated.

"I would love to get your comments," Harriet responded.

"What else have you been up to?" Margaret asked.

"Not much. The paper is taking most of my time. If I want a break I distribute flyers for Leonard Brown."

"I had a dinner for some of his donors not long ago. We viewed several new television ads his staff produced."

"I watched a new one yesterday at the annex. The tech guys think it will be a real blow to the Wilson campaign."

"Oh?" Margaret questioned.

"It's a recording in his own words. They installed a fiber optic recorder in his home and got him and the prime minister in a very candid discussion, talking about illegal immigrants and deals with Iran and kickbacks from contractors. Wilson was even talking about using a program to spy on people. It's supposed to be ready for distribution in a couple of days. They gave me a preliminary copy to show Scott."

"If you have it with you we could watch it here."

"I didn't take it to the airport. It's at my house," she replied. "I was going to watch it with him when he takes me home."

"Well let's leave it like that," Margaret added. "I'm having another dinner for our donors soon. Maybe I'll see it then."

"If they haven't finished it by now, it should be ready before long," Harriet said.

"I hope this time they can show the kind of person James Wilson has become; he has to win no matter the cost."

Sandra was cleaning the table and interrupted their talk to ask if they wanted anything else. They both declined, and she removed the tableware to a nearby cart.

"I hope I didn't upset you, talking about the video," Harriet said. "I'm happy to change the subject."

"It's not that, Harriet," Margaret replied. "It's just when it comes to him I'm intolerant. I've experienced his methods; he's exploitive and vindictive, and he gets his support from naïve, generous people who believe his rhetoric and don't realize they're being used to serve his ends."

"His name comes up in my gerrymandering thesis too."

"That doesn't surprise me," Margaret stated.

Scott returned to the patio and said, "Well, mother, I think it's time Harriet and I were on our way."

"Well, this was nice; try not to be so long between visits."

"Mother, every time I come to visit or call you're gone."

"My group property meeting was canceled today or you would have missed me this time too."

"See what I mean," he replied.

"Call me anytime, but not Sunday morning. That's still reserved for worship services."

"What church do you go to, Ms. Farrow?" Harriet asked.

"UCA, on McClaren Street. But sometimes we'll have prayer services here."

"Say a few prayers for me, mother," Scott said in good conscience.

"You know I do, Scott," she stated with candor.

"Goodbye, Ms. Farrow," said Harriet.

"When are you going to start calling me Margaret?"

Harriet smiled, "Goodbye, Margaret."

Scott kissed her again, and they waved goodbye.

 Ronald Lutz

"How about we go to my place?" Harriet suggested with a broad smile as they walked to the car.

"You took the words right out of my mouth," he said, also smiling as they turned and waved to Sandra.

———

Sandra was one of three personal attendants employed by Margaret and currently on duty from mid-afternoon until late evening. Nancy Day worked early morning to mid-afternoon and Beatrice Pierson worked the night shift. Each month the women rotated their assignments. They carried out needed chores when Margaret was away from the estate. A bedroom and all the facilities of the home were available for their use when they were not needed elsewhere.

Beatrice and Nancy had worked for Margaret from the time she became disabled. Sandra had been hired recently to replace a long-time employee who retired. All three women maintained homes a distance from Balmoral. Beatrice was a sixty-four-year-old widow with no family and was grudgingly anticipating retirement in the next year. Nancy was forty-five, divorced, and the mother of two children in their twenties. Sandra was thirty-two and married to a New South Wales Judicial Commissioner, Edward Morse. They were parents of an eleven-year-old son.

Due to their length of employment, Beatrice and Nancy had a comfortable relationship with Margaret. But Sandra was still getting used to working at the estate. Each day had its challenges, but things seemed to be slowly improving.

After Harriet and Scott drove away, Sandra removed the dish cart from the patio and returned later to find Margaret trying to concentrate on the corporate reports.

"It was nice to see Scott again," Sandra said to her. "You must be happy his trip to Indonesia went so well."

"Yes, he's doing just fine," Margaret responded.

"Do you think he's really serious about Harriet?" Sandra questioned. "After all, he would be attractive to any number of other young women."

Margaret looked pensively at Sandra and said, "Let's let him decide that for himself, shall we?"

Ronald Lutz

CHAPTER FIVE

At the age of fifty-seven James Wilson was, arguably, still at the peak of his political prowess. Standing five feet, eleven inches tall, he was a portly man with a pockmarked face, and his brown hair was graying at the sides. A chain-smoker, he went through several packs of Winfield 25s each day and had lately been using reading glasses. Raised in the country town of Jamberoo, one hundred kilometers south of Sydney, he was the first person in his family to attend college, that by way of a general scholarship, at Macquarie University. He utilized the grant to pursue a dual major studying political science and law and achieved success in both disciplines by the use of skillful strategies rather than by a scholarly approach. Curious about stories of the rich and powerful, he charted a path from rags to riches by forming a close relationship with Margaret Farrow, a Macquarie classmate and only child of Danforth Farrow, the most wealthy, prestigious man in Australia. The object of affection of many gentlemen callers, Margaret preferred one of her other classmates, Ray Dowling. They were inseparable until he left school to work as a volunteer in Africa.

During Dowling's three year absence Wilson used a charm campaign to develop a rapport with Margaret and his alluring persistence eventually won her over. They graduated in the same class and were married within a month, to the chagrin of her mother who hoped she would follow the desires of her deceased husband and wait for Ray to return.

Wilson enriched his career, relying on the wealth and good name of Danforth Farrow. However, after his untimely death, the benefit derived from the Farrow name gradually faded and could not be counted on to contribute to Wilson's future ambitions. He became a career politician, spending the first five of his thirty-five years as a union steward on the Sydney docks during his time in college. While practicing law after graduation he took a position as Parliament staffer for one of the representatives to his home state of New South Wales. He stayed with the law firm for a brief time but soon declared his candidacy as a national Representative for the Labor ticket and won the seat in his first try at the age of thirty. Charismatic and persuasive, he culled the favor of a cadre of prominent legislators and six years later was elected to the Senate.

When he reached age forty-two he had become opposition leader for the minority party. Three years later his party swept the elections; he was chosen leader of the Senate by his peers. So from the age of forty-five, with continued backing from his political base, he remained Senate majority leader, ensuring his support by pushing through legislation his constituents favored. The oldest senator in parliament was considered to be the party leader, but James Wilson, in his current position, was recognized as the most powerful man in government.

However, a repulsive pattern of lies and criminality came to dominate his life personally and politically. He began to rely on a more sinister behavior that transformed his charm into an abusive personality; his womanizing became well known, and he often entertained and seduced women. Confrontation by Margaret about his activities produced no contrition. Instead, Wilson aggressively pointed out what he saw as noticeable indiscretions centered around her affection for Ray Dowling. He knew she had been seeing him. He had returned to Sydney from Africa and accepted a job as a local radio station host and political pundit.

In order to keep a watchful eye on Dowling, Wilson hired him for a campaign post and soon came to realize he was the best political operative in New South Wales. Though they disliked one another, their work produced notable successes.

 Ronald Lutz

Wilson became sadistic. But earlier, he had spearheaded several notable environmental bills as a new representative to politics and worked on a committee calling for infrastructure changes while chairing an economics and industry board. Introduced to men of wealth and power on that board, Wilson strove to emulate their lifestyle, and his increased community standing following his marriage inflamed his appetite; he began to imitate their business practices.

He invested in commercial enterprises as a silent partner. One such venture, Sea Charter Tours, helped him stay in touch with everything that was happening on the waterfront. Over the years, he was able to establish a far-reaching, influential network—a system that relied on threats and intimidation and attracted a syndicate of professional and political agents eager to carry out his bidding. His chosen methodology developed to include exploitation, bribery, and, on occasion, murder.

The media touted his political achievements but as his approach to political expediency became more alarming, they were inclined to look the other way, minimizing bad press while supporting his agenda. And they did not report on his domestic troubles that eventually led to divorce.

Returning home one day, Wilson pulled into the garage unobserved and watched Dowling leave the house. Wasting no time, he accused Margaret of having an affair, confronting her in the bedroom. Her vehement denials increased his rage. She broke away from his insults and strode across the second-story landing; he followed her to the top of the stairs. When she started to descend the staircase, he stepped on her robe.

His action was deliberate and purposeful, causing her to have a crippling fall. She didn't know he was the cause until Scott, thirteen at the time, told her he witnessed what had happened. He ran from his room to help her; he never forgave his father.

The divorce proceedings dragged on for a year. Wilson continued with his accusations and denied any responsibility for the "accident." In the end, she accepted a court judgment of irreconcilable differences. There was no cash settlement. No longer dependent on her inherited wealth, he also accepted the ruling of the court. Meanwhile, Dowling worked to fulfill his contract with Wilson and then returned to the radio before joining the Brown campaign.

————

Elections for November had been called and preliminary polls showed Wilson slightly ahead of Leonard Brown, much closer than Wilson expected. However, he took nothing for granted and would use any method to secure an advantage and maintain his lead. When he learned a video jeopardizing his candidacy had been produced by the Brown campaign, he assigned several devoted cronies the task of preventing its release and circulation while supervising the removal of all the fiber optic devices from his home. Then he attended an evening campaign rally promoting his candidacy. It was an event he might normally skip, but due to what was planned for that October 3 evening he thought it best to attend. The rally was at a location where he could be seen by all.

Ronald Lutz

CHAPTER SIX

— October 4 —

A ringing telephone early Friday morning roused David Haggerty from a dreamless sleep. He groped for his cell phone on the bedside table even as the sound went quiet. His wife, Susan, a chronic insomniac, was sitting up in bed and clutched a woman's magazine in one hand while passing a corded phone receiver to him across her body with the other.

"It's Brian," she said as he pushed himself to a sitting position and took the phone. "He said he tried to call your cell, but it went to voice mail. You must have turned it off."

"Yeah," he replied to Brian as he reached for pen and pad.

He cupped the phone between his shoulder and jaw, "Okay ...got it." He handed the receiver back to his wife.

"Where at?" she asked, hanging up the phone and sliding to a prone position.

"Marrickville."

He crawled out of bed and smoothed the sheet next to her. She rolled over on her left side while clutching the magazine and was sound asleep before he finished dressing.

They both grew up in Parramatta but had not met until they attended Western Sydney University. Married nineteen years, they lived all that time in the same house financed by the local bank. She had been known for her beauty queen looks—she was high school prom queen—and the most popular girl in school before attending college. At Western Sydney, she participated in local talent shows, the theater, and cheerleading and found time to study secondary education. He was a criminology major and first noticed her red hair, green eyes, and shapely form when she cheered for the soccer crew. He was the team captain and won her heart, although she had many suitors. After dating two years, they married and he put money down on their house. Following college, she accepted a teaching position in a nearby preschool despite being tormented by the onset of an anxiety disorder, a contributing factor to a substantial increase in weight she gained over time. A correct diagnosis of her disorder and the right medication helped her lose all but twenty excess pounds. Their twin daughters, Angela and Christine, were in secondary school. Spanky was the pet cocker spaniel.

David pulled on his slacks, shoes, and a white shirt. Then he strapped on a shoulder holster containing his SIG Sauer P226 police gun. Last of all, he slipped on a charcoal-gray police jacket, and then checked himself in a mirror before grabbing a suit coat and tie and a digital camera. He was six feet, two inches tall with straight light brown hair and hazel eyes; he had kept in shape since his academy days. After turning out Susan's bed light, he left the house and input the street address given to him by Brian into his Chrysler Commodore police car GPS system. The car was his to use since earning the rank of inspector two years earlier. His downtown office was thirty-five kilometers distant, but the Marrickville address was half that distance. After getting coffee to go from an all-night diner, he arrived at 2:00 a.m. and parked behind an ambulance and three police cars, one of which had begun to drive away. The home was cordoned off with police tape; the front door was open and the house bathed in light. Several nearby homes had their lights on, and he saw one person across the street looking from inside their home through a front window. He got out of the car and a uniformed policeman met him.

"Hi, Dave."

"Chuck," David said with familiarity. "They inside?"

"Yeah. Looks like he shot the woman and then himself."

"Okay, let's have a look." David grabbed his digital camera and the two men walked slowly to the house. Two other officers in their cars and the men in the ambulance continued to wait at the curb.

"Anything outside?" David asked as they walked to the house.

"Nothin' that we could find."

They went in the front door and Chuck pointed toward the bedroom. David looked at the walls and carpet as they walked slowly to where the two bodies lay on the floor.

"Any other places in the house disturbed?"

"No," Chuck said. "It looks like it all took place right here. She lived here—rented. The owner lives in Revesby. This guy," he pointed to the dead man, "had an apartment in Surry Hills. He must have come in, confronted her, and that was it."

David nodded his head to say he understood.

"The front door and one of the doors to the deck were both open when we got here," Chuck continued.

"Looks like an expensive ring she's got on," David remarked. "Nice looking girl."

"Yeah, if you like chocolate," Chuck interposed.

David gave him a noncommittal glance.

"Doesn't figure he'd be her fella," David said. "He must be twice her age."

"Ya' never know these days," Chuck responded.

"Were you able to ID them?"

"There's a license in his wallet—Raymond Dowling," Chuck said.

"Was there money in it?" David asked.

"Fifty-nine dollars," replied Chuck. "There's other cash and jewelry here too."

"So money, jewelry, and her ring. Probably rules out robbery."

"How 'bout the woman?" David asked.

Chuck looked at his notepad: "Harriet White."

"Anything more?"

"Nothing yet," he answered while shaking his head no.

"When was it called in?" David asked.

"The ambulance got an anonymous call after nine. They called us about ten. Brian and I got here about eleven."

"What's that, pieces of a compact disc?" David asked.

"Yeah. We figured maybe he found a video of her with another man and he couldn't handle it," Chuck stated. "We got most of the pieces to the lab, but it's too smashed up to piece back together. Brian took pictures and made a video. He was leaving when you drove up."

"Looks like she was only shot once," commented David.

"Only two bullets were fired," added Chuck.

"The gun looks like a Sig Sauer," David suggested.

"Yeah. Almost like the one we use," said Chuck.

"Okay. I'll take a couple more pictures."

After they checked the bodies again, David released them to the recently arrived coroner and the waiting ambulance. Then he went through the house. He found nothing significant to the crime but took a framed photograph of Scott found in the bedroom and left the house, arriving at his office at 4:00 a.m.

Jennifer slipped out of bed unclothed and threw on a blue, cotton dress with buttons down the front. Stopping at a mirror to comb her hair, she observed Mike through the looking glass staring at her as he rested in bed. She thought the impassive gaze on his face was unusual since they had just been intimate.

"Are you going for the interview?" she asked, switching to a brush to style her hair while looking at him in the mirror.

He didn't answer, so she put the brush down and went to his side of the bed. "It's a good opportunity," she remarked.

He mumbled a noncommittal response.

"I'll make some coffee," she purred. "It's almost eight. You kept me in bed way too long" and leaning over, she gave him a quick kiss on the cheek, then went to the kitchen.

As he lay in bed, thoughts of his life and his wife and their relationship began to percolate like the coffee in the kitchen.

He was the only child of Harold and Lydia Denham. His parents lived in south Sydney near Glen Alpine when he was young, but his father had taken a job as a marine attendant and worked as a boat detailer and mechanic before investing in a boat of his own and running a small tourist fishing business. However, his mother died at an early age. Always in poor health from the time he could remember, she passed away of a congenital heart disease when he was five. His father never remarried and died of a stroke soon after turning seventy years old, three years ago when Mike was forty years of age. In his teen years, he worked in the summer with his father. The rest of the year he attended Thomas Reddall public high school in Glen Alpine, but skipped his final year, and a promising relationship with Jennifer, to enlist in the Royal Australian Navy. He felt he was ready for anything the navy had to offer.

He and Jennifer dated in school and their time together led to intimacy. Then he walked away without even a cursory goodbye. Jennifer had tugged on his sleeve, but not hard enough to change his plans. RAN had become his dream. He would get paid, learn a skill, and if it worked out, establish a vocation and retire in twenty years with full benefits. Unfortunately, there were too many rules and regulations to suit him. After completing a three-year assignment, achieving the rank of helmsman, he chose not to reenlist. He decided his training had made him ready to operate his own vessel.

However, after leaving the navy, it would be a full ten years knocking around on cargo boats and charter operations before he finally was hired to take the helm of the new superyacht *Serendipitous*. He figured his earnings would allow him to save enough money over the next several years to get his own boat. He was thirty years old at that time and had not lost his love for the sea; any thoughts of marriage rarely, if ever, entered his mind. When Jennifer came aboard he had been captain for two years.

How ya' doin'. His greeting poured out like warm honey. *Mike Denham's the name. Glad ya' came.* As the captain, his welcome to the reporter was intended to be casual and friendly, but his words had barely been spoken before he recognized the girl from their high school days, Jennifer Akston. She had been a year junior to him. He first noticed her when their classes began to intermix in secondary school. Besides her good looks and charm, what had appealed to him more than anything was her robust, yet very feminine, laugh. But she was not disposed to laugh as she boarded the *Serendipitous*; recognizing him, her smile faded into solicitous, pursed lips. Later, after agreeing to drinks and dinner, they began to see the possibility of reuniting again and a new relationship. He realized she had, literally, walked back into his life. They came to value their time together, bonding romantically - emotionally and intellectually - and in their lovemaking. Their commitment to one another grew; they came to appreciate the strengths each one possessed but did not overlook pointing out certain weaknesses when necessary.

He had one extended voyage in the next few months, making it possible for them to be together often. Within a year of their reunion on the superyacht they married, ending his command on the vessel. He soon signed on with Carnival Cruise Lines as third officer aboard the ship *Spirit* on its Sydney to New Zealand run and quickly worked his way up to staff captain.

By his third year with Carnival, he was on a path to be captain and was home every ten days for several days at a time until the ship added a thirty-two day round trip voyage to Singapore. Jennifer was not pleased. Before they married she had voiced many concerns about how often he would be gone. With the change in his cruise requirements, he could no longer assure her of plenty of shore time. Adding to her displeasure and their difficulties, she was unable to conceive during their first years together. Reluctantly, at her insistence, he agreed to quit his position at Carnival and sign on with a local cruise tour operating out of Sydney Harbour. His take-home pay was slashed, but at least he was still working on the sea. They often argued but seldom paid attention to what the other said.

Finally, he'd had enough; he walked out on their marriage. But

     Ronald Lutz

unlike their high school days, he was thinking of her all the time and realized his love for her was still strong. Apart for a year, he began to wonder if she could forgive him for walking out on her again. They reunited, and after that their partnership seemed to be on a stable footing. That all changed when he read the email; it was obvious she had become involved with another man. It had been almost a week since he read it. Why hadn't he confronted her with what he knew?

Jennifer was raised in Campelltown City in the suburb of Glen Alpine. Her parents still lived in their family home. Her father was close to retirement from his elected position on the Campelltown City Council, having been reelected to that position five times. His one attempt to become mayor had not been successful. Her mother had been teaching close to home at Ambarvale Public School for almost thirty years.

Jennifer had twin sisters and a brother. They were in their mid-thirties and no longer lived in New South Wales. Her sisters had both taken jobs in Cairns; one sister worked in a tourist office, and the other was a chef in a restaurant. Her brother had moved to Perth five years earlier to supervise a landscape and gardening service. Since Jennifer lived only sixty kilometers from her parents' home she visited them often, and the rest of the family usually met together for holidays, except for her brother who was able to visit only occasionally.

A reporter for almost twenty years, Jennifer loved the work and its challenges. After graduating from the University of Wollongong with a bachelor of arts in journalism she first worked four years as an urban writer at the *Morning Herald*. Hiring on with the *Daily Telegraph*, she began as a beat reporter, moved to entertainment reporter, and then political correspondent.

A promotion to her current job, investigative reporter, soon followed. She had remained in print journalism, although more than a few colleagues thought her attractive features and blonde hair made her a candidate for TV broadcast news anchorwoman.

While she was in the kitchen making coffee her cell phone rang. Sidney Presser, a beat reporter for the paper, had been checking the downtown police wire to get information on breaking stories. He was calling to ask if she wanted to follow up on a murder-suicide. She had seen the breaking news report on the kitchen TV minutes before and agreed to look into it, hesitating only a moment when told David Haggerty was the officer in charge. After a hurried shower, she put on a modest blue pencil skirt, short-sleeved button-down white polyester top, two-inch navy pumps, and a thin gem pendant necklace, an anniversary gift from Mike. Other than a wedding ring she usually wore very little jewelry. Mike was taking his turn in the bathroom when she left, so she shouted a goodbye and hurried off to the Goulburn Street police station.

It was a short drive for her from their home to the *Daily Telegraph*. The police station was nearby, and she arrived at 9:15 a.m. for a morning appointment.

Entering the recently updated headquarter building, she noted the well-lit lobby and high open ceiling; the floor was white porcelain tile and the waiting area had new furniture.

A newsroom, meeting room, and the waiting area were near the entrance. Behind a reception desk, cubicle workstations and several private offices on the back wall occupied the space. Approaching the desk sergeant, Jennifer confirmed a meeting with Haggerty and waited ten minutes before being ushered into one of the back rooms. The office appeared bigger than it was because of its off-white urban carpet, high ceiling, and the large back window with a panoramic view of the city. It was modestly furnished with a desk, filing cabinet, table, and two chairs. Haggerty, seated behind his desk, got up and motioned for her to sit in a chair across from him.

"How have you been?" he asked as they both sat down.

He continued on as she nodded affirmatively.

"Heard you were promoted. Congratulations."

"Thanks. I see you've moved up too," she offered.

"How 'bout this view?" he suggested.

     Ronald Lutz

"Much better than in my office," she responded.

"Well ...so what brings you here?" he asked.

"Marrickville," she spoke out pointedly.

"Oh, well, there's not much to investigate," he said.

"Except, if what Sid told me is right, it was a mixed-race couple and both worked for the Brown campaign," she probed.

"We don't know yet if they were a couple," he said. "Apparently the man worked for Brown; she was a volunteer."

"Okay, but a murder-suicide always gets the attention of my readers. Who were the victims?" she asked.

"Raymond Dowling and Harriet White," he stated. "Next of kin haven't been notified, so don't use their names yet."

"Okay. Anything else my readers can sink their teeth in over their morning coffee?" she asked.

"We've got a gun."

"Wait! Did you say Dowling? The same Dowling that worked for James Wilson, the Senate leader?" she asked.

"I don't know," Haggerty responded.

"If he is, that's noteworthy," she said. "He used to work for Wilson and now he was with the Brown campaign."

There was a momentary pause as Jennifer considered it.

"Do you want to know about the gun?" Haggerty asked.

"Of course," she stated.

"It was a SIG Sauer Mosquito. Similar to one I use."

"Anything else?" she asked.

"How about a video of the crime scene?" he offered.

"Sure, maybe I'll spot a clue. Any lab reports yet?"

"We'll get them tomorrow or Monday," he said.

"I may follow-up to see if there's anything newsworthy," she said as he reached in his desk for the video. He handed it to her and she stood up and stepped toward the door.

"I meant to contact you before now," he remarked, "to apologize for taking advantage of you when ...we were together."

"What do you mean?" she asked.

"Just that I know you and Mike were on the outs. But as it happened, my wife and I had some issues too."

"Oh." She sat down again on the edge of the chair.

"Her classroom work fell off. So did her teacher ratings. She was working too hard while trying to care for our girls."

"I've often wondered how mothers are able to do that."

"It didn't help that she gained a lot of weight," Haggerty added. "It wasn't a pleasant time. I should have been more patient but instead of dealing with it I chose to, well..."

"I understand. We were both vulnerable."

"Yeah. Well, she's a lot better now. She's lost a lot of that weight. Still got some to go, though," he said, smiling. "I saw a counselor and we both took a stress management course. It helped quite a bit."

"I'm happy you're both doing better," she said, standing up again. "Thanks, David, and thanks for the video. I won't keep it long."

On her way out she stopped at a water cooler to consider what turned out to be a less stressful reintroduction to David Haggerty than she expected. How long had it been, over four years? Now, as an investigator, she probably should be prepared to see him more often. She walked to her car, thankful for her loving relationship with her husband.

CHAPTER SEVEN

air winds and following seas escorted a luxury yacht into Broken Bay Harbour late one evening. The ship reduced speed and moved slowly toward a preassigned docking berth at the Royal Motor Yacht Club, almost forty kilometers north of Sydney. The six-year-old vessel was in first-rate shape from fore to aft and could easily accommodate up to ten passengers; four lower deck staterooms, a saloon on the main deck, and a lounge topside met the needs of anyone on board.

Before daybreak the next day, activity had intensified in and around the ship. The batteries were tested for a full charge, water and fuel capacities were replenished, and the interior and exterior had both been cleaned and polished. In less than ten hours the yacht had been equipped for service and could have passed a rigorous inspection; everything was ship-shape and a final operational test of the engines proved the ship was ready for service. She was destined to soon return to the sea.

The Friday lunch crowd jammed the sidewalk on Circular Quay as Jim Foster, pushing sixty years old and walking with a pronounced limp, hurried toward the harbor master offices. Dressed in work clothes, he looked out of place among the men wearing suits. About five feet, six inches tall, he had a thick, muscular frame that was stocky but not overweight; his unkempt hair and bushy eyebrows were gray and he sported a two-day stubble beard. For the last ten years he had rented a room in the home of his younger sister and her husband in Lavender Bay, across the Harbour Bridge north of downtown. Having worked all his life on boats and around the docks at Sydney Harbour he was known to be honest and forthright, but his dream of being an independent operator had long been off his wish list. Currently, he was working for a Dutch shipping line unloading cargo from one of their scows. That morning after parking his old Ford coupe in a lot close to the work site his day was immediately interrupted by a man with an offer: James Wilson would pay him five hundred dollars if he could find someone who could take a yacht to Malaysia.

Foster and Wilson first met years before on a fishing boat that operated day excursions; a freak accident one day caused Foster to suffer his leg injury. Wilson, a novice seaman, was working to earn spending money in his second year of college. When he leaned over the rail to pull in a fishing net, a tourist lost his balance and careened across the deck toward him. In his distracted state of mind, the tourist failed to drop the filet knife clutched in his hand. Foster intercepted him and pushed the blade down so Wilson was not hit. However, it pierced Foster's shin, rupturing a tendon, tearing a good portion of leg muscle, and caused a significant loss of blood. Wilson believed he had been saved from a similar fate, if not worse, and respected what Foster had done. Not often holding others in esteem, Wilson adhered to a code that honored those who earned his favor, Foster being one of them.

Over the years, he was contacted periodically by Wilson to locate a dock worker or relay instructions to a boat operator. Foster never questioned the motive; he never had a reason to suspect anything sinister or problematic, and he was always well paid. Early on Wilson had given him a smartphone to make it easy to stay in touch, but invariably he forgot to turn it on or even carry it with him. It was off the previous night and that morning. Wilson sent out several men to find a yacht operator, but a few others were also told to look for Foster. Wilson figured he was his best bet to find a helmsman. When Foster was told about the five hundred dollars he informed his cargo

    Ronald Lutz

boss he could not work that day and then was driven to the Grace Hotel to see Wilson in his suite and get the details.

Wilson told him he sold the yacht to a buyer in Malacca, Malaysia—half down, half on delivery. Terms of the sale, the vessel, and a major compensation for the operator were all discussed. As an afterthought, Wilson added that the yacht had to leave Sydney that night. It was then Foster realized the three hundred dollar wage he would have earned working on the scow that day would have been the better, smarter choice.

However, upon leaving Wilson's suite he thought of Mike Denham. He made several calls from the hotel lobby trying to track Mike down and learned he was at the harbor master headquarters for a job interview.

Foster had worked as a deckhand for Mike three years on two different yachts and knew he was an excellent helmsman. He was disciplined, responsible, and single-minded—certain people would say stubborn—about how things were to be run. They were important qualities for every ship captain. Foster knew Mike's compass was always on the right heading. But more than that, he knew Mike was out of work, having been fired from Sea Charter Tours recently as a disciplinary action. The circumstances were somewhat vague.

Foster had walked more than a mile from the Grace Hotel to get to the harbor master headquarters and his left leg, scarred due to the boating accident those many years earlier, was throbbing. As he neared the building he saw Denham coming outside through its central revolving door. He was wearing khaki pants, a light green shirt, dark tie, dark brown blazer, and brown loafers. Mike looked around indecisively and saw Foster wave at him, signaling for him to stop and talk.

Beads of perspiration were forming on Foster's forehead, though it was only 21°C. He greeted Mike.

"Hullo. Been lookin' for you."

"What's up?" Denham replied.

"Heard you lost the Charter job," Foster stated. "Figur'd somethin' else 'ud come along, like harbor master," he hesitated, "...but if you wanta try somethin' else, I thought you might think 'bout takin' a yacht to Malaysia."

"Don't have one," Denham said with jocular sarcasm. "Besides, I'll have this job come next week."

Foster ignored his comment. "The one I'm thinkin' of is like one a' them motor yachts up at Woolrich. It'd pay better than harbor intern and start right away." He paused, "Be good ta' get on one a' them ocean yachts agin, don't ya' figur'?"

"Don't think on it too much," Mike said.

"It'd be like those ya' used to operate," Foster suggested.

Mike responded indifferently. "Will ya' quit beatin' 'round the bush and tell me what it is you're tryin' ta' say?"

"I could drink somethin'," Foster said. "How 'bout buyin' me a beer; talk better that way. There's a pub over near where my car's parked."

They small-talked their way to the crowded tavern, got a table, and ordered some beer before Foster resumed his pitch.

"A fella' I know got in touch with me 'bout a motor yacht he sold to a friend in Malaysia. He's lookin' for someone ta' take her there. Seems the guy who used to run her moved to New Zealand awhile back and our fella' can't take the time to run her up there himself. That's it in a nutshell."

"What makes ya' think I'd be interested?" Mike asked.

"Cause a' your situation, and cause it's a sweet deal."

"How sweet?" Mike responded.

"Our fella' will pay a hundred thousand, plus expenses, ta' anyone who can get her up there," Foster said.

"That ain't chump change. Why aren't you jumpin' to do it?" Mike asked.

"You know I'm no yachtsman, and I got this bum leg."

"Where is the yacht?" Mike asked.

"Royal Yacht Club." Foster sipped his beverage. "I'll take you there and you can check it out."

 Ronald Lutz

"How big is she?

"Thirty meters," Foster responded. "You'd need a couple a' hands. Plus this fella' wants his son to go along ta' guard the investment. He'll pay all expenses. The yacht's all ready to go but ya' gotta get underway by midnight tonight."

"You gotta be kidding!" Mike reacted with disbelief.

"You'll get a ten thousand dollar bonus if you leave by then. Seems our fella's fightin' a nuisance order on another boat and thinks the State might seize the yacht as payment."

"A guy with a yacht like what you're talkin' about and he won't fork over an impound fee?" Mike declared.

"You know how these fellas are. It's somethin' personal, you can bet that." Foster stated. All I know is if you don't go tonight, he fig'urs she'll be impounded. Then likely he'll lose the sale and you'll be out a hundred grand."

Denham, skeptical, "What am I missin'?"

"Look, I heard you were outta work; fig'urd you could use the money. If you're interested..." Foster laid out ten one hundred dollar bills on the table. "That's a thousand and you'll get nine more if ya' leave afore midnight."

Mike pondered the cash on the table. "I'd need some kinda' guarantee that I get paid. You got a contract?"

"I'll get one when I get the other nine thousand," Foster offered. What d'ya say?"

"You say the other guy pays expenses?"

"Yeah, his son. You ain't on the cuff for nothin'. You'll even get airfare home," Foster answered.

Mike looked at him, hesitated, and then took the money.

A voyage of considerable distance was hastily arranged. Once the money changed hands, Foster left the pub to get the rest of the money and a contract. They agreed to meet in one hour at the harbor master steps near the "Rocks" from where Foster would drive them to the yacht club. After the two men parted, Mike placed a call to see if he could get a crew.

"Ronnie? Mike. I'm takin' a yacht to Malaysia; gotta leave tonight. Can you and Joel go?"

He laughed at the response, then continued,

"Haven't seen her yet; she's at the Royal Yacht Club; thirty meters. Bring your passports and go to my place and get mine, bottom right-hand desk drawer. And get my brown duffel in the bedroom. Call me when you get to the club, and I'll direct you to her. See ya."

He made a second call to his wife, but not to her cell number; he didn't want to try and explain a cruise of several weeks, especially after interviewing with the harbor master. Instead, he recorded a voice mail message to their home phone. He also called the harbor master office and withdrew his name for consideration of the intern position.

Foster met him an hour or so later and brought the rest of the down payment and a notarized contract signed by the owner of the yacht, James Wilson. Mike nodded his approval after examining the contract, unaware Wilson was the silent partner responsible for his dismissal at Sea Charter. But Foster withheld the money, saying he was told not to pay the rest until Wilson's son was on board. He then drove the two of them north of Sydney to where the yacht was docked at the yacht club. After a lengthy inspection, Mike agreed the yacht was prepped and looked to be ready to go. Ronnie and Joel arrived at about twilight time.

———

Jennifer sat at her desk in the newsroom of the Sydney *Daily Telegraph*. Since being promoted months earlier the promise of her own private office had remained unfulfilled. She was stuck in the same cubicle she had always occupied, in the center of a large room full of cubicles trying with difficulty to focus on the

     Ronald Lutz

crime video Haggerty loaned her, but her thoughts were on Mike and the interview he had with the harbor master. It was late Friday afternoon. She thought he would call to tell her how it went.

From her point of view, the opening for a career position as Sydney harbor master was an ideal opportunity for Mike. When the posting for the position first appeared in the paper, his qualifications seemed to be in line with the job description. She tried to offer encouragement by reminding him of his goal to buy a boat and start his own company. She argued, as the harbor master, it wouldn't take long to start earning money again to add to his meager savings. But he had to convince them at the interview that he wanted the job.

Recently, over the last week or so, she thought Mike seemed to be going through the motions. When they dated in high school she fell in love with him and thought of him as being self-assured and dependable, until he left without a word to join the navy.

It took several relationships before her love for him faded. Years later, when she worked as a beat reporter at the paper, they met again. Her assignment editor asked her to do a human interest story about the superyacht *Serendipitous* anchored in Sydney Harbour. Captain Mike Denham, still poised, still self-assured, met her when she boarded the yacht and almost immediately their relationship was reignited. They were married before long, but the bond they formed began to unravel over time although not in a dramatic way. It wasn't that he was uncaring or abusive, but he was no longer the attentive, eager-to-please man she knew from the first few years of their marriage; he had become distant and restrained in both his attitude and his lovemaking. He was unhappy. She wondered if his unhappiness was like the way she felt when he left her to join the navy.

"I worked up a draft on Marrickville while you were with Haggerty." She was startled back to the present by her co-worker. "Can we print the names of the victims yet?"

"No. Still no next of kin."

Dennis Williams had broken her reverie. He was typing an

online story on his computer across the aisle from where she sat. He wore linen pants, an open-collared striped shirt, and Brooks shoes and was gnawing on a round wooden toothpick.

Of the three people assigned to Jennifer's fact-finding unit, Dennis was the person she counted on most. Thirty years old and recently married, he had been with the *Telegraph* less than four years but proved to be the best of her three contributors.

Now she was trying to decide if Marrickville was a story worth investigating. One of the victims, Raymond Dowling, had been chief of staff to James Wilson for a number of years, but few readers would probably recall him or his role when he worked for the Wilson campaign. His passing should warrant only a "page 6" insert, but because he and the woman who died with him had both been working with the Leonard Brown campaign, political intrigue might hype the story. She also wondered if Dowling's political party switch could have caused the murder-suicide. With that in mind, she decided to follow-up on the story; it was worth further inquiry, and Dennis was there to help.

"Are they calling it domestic violence?" he asked.

"All I know," she answered, "is they both worked for the Brown campaign."

He turned his chair toward her. "Did you know they had a fire at their headquarters last night?"

"I heard; I linked it to our story. That's all I've got done other than stare at this crime scene video."

"Where did you get that?" he asked with incredulity.

"Haggerty." She flashed a playful grin at Dennis. "It's the one for Marrickville; I didn't even have to ask for it."

"He gave it to you, just like that?"

She arched an eyebrow and gave him a sideways look.

"But won't he get in trouble?"

Jennifer smiled. "Not if he doesn't get caught."

Dennis smiled too, then turned back and continued to type. Jennifer was scrolling the Internet for information about the victims; she knew Ray Dowling from her time as a political reporter. Dennis remembered his name too.

"Didn't Dowling have some political clout at one time?"

"Until several years ago he was chief of staff for James Wilson, the Labor leader." Jennifer abruptly sat up straight and asked Dennis to look at an Internet picture on her computer: a photo of three men standing in front of a yacht.

"Talk about political clout," she remarked. "Look at the caption: 'Three prominent Labor leaders.'"

"That's Barnes, isn't it?" he questioned.

"Prime Minister Barnes, Dowling, and ...James Wilson. Taken four years ago. About the time Dowling moved on."

"There's your in-depth. Interview Barnes," he said.

"He's in Melbourne, but Wilson's got a press office not far from here." She called their number and shook her head no at Dennis when a recorded message was heard.

"I'll call them on Monday," she said, removing the police video from the computer. "I should have called them earlier instead of daydreaming."

Dennis, typing again. "Do you know what gun was used?"

"A SIG Sauer Mosquito. The police use it."

"Who reported it to the ambulance?" he asked, typing.

"Mr. Anonymous," she replied.

"Probably a neighbor. They never want to get involved."

"You wonder why it happens," she stated thoughtfully.

"Maybe the guy wanted to settle an old score."

It was past five o'clock on Friday and she was ready to leave. She asked him to forward his story to her computer at home so she could read it. Dennis was ready to go, too, but was waiting for a computer backup program to finish.

"You be in tomorrow?" he asked, as she left her cubicle.

"What do you think? I'm a regular weekend warrior."

———

THE DENHAMS HAD LIVED IN THE INNER WEST NEIGHBORHOOD
of Glebe for seven years. The short commute for Jennifer to the
Daily Telegraph in the central business district took about fifteen
minutes. Tonight, rather than drive straight home, she took a detour
to Marrickville to see the house where the crime occurred. The
scene seemed pleasant enough: a ranch-style home on the corner
lot of a cul-de-sac with a manicured lawn and a hedge on the side.

Crime tape still surrounded the area, and a police car was in
front of the house. Stopping the car on Newburry, a street crossing
Pine Street, she tried to imagine the interior of the home from the
police video. It was a useless exercise.

She returned to Glebe. A shopping district with stores, restaurants, and other services was nearby, and she stopped at a market
and purchased two frozen entrées and the makings for a salad
before going home. By the time she arrived at their house on Darling Street, near Blackwattle Bay, it was dark. She and Mike had
lived in an apartment after they married but moved to Glebe—the
house location and mortgage rate suited them. The property had
since gained in value considerably.

Mike relied primarily on public transportation to get around;
a light rail station was a few hundred yards from their house. But
Jennifer was driving a new Toyota Corolla, a reward to herself following her promotion. Arriving home from the store, she parked
under the carport. A motion detector light prompted her yellow
cat, Snoopy, to enter the house by the cat door. Jennifer carried the
few items she purchased into the kitchen and placed them on the
table. There was no note, the lights were off, and it was very quiet.
Obviously, Mike was not home. She put the entrées in the freezer
and got out a can of Meow Meal for Snoopy.

Turning on the lights, she walked through the rest of the house—
front room, living room, and bedrooms. Was Mike's duffel gone? She
was sure it had been there that morning. Retracing her steps, she
stopped in the front room at the desk to look for a note. The red light
on the answering machine was blinking and indicated there were

 Ronald Lutz

two messages waiting. She couldn't remember the last time they had received a message on the machine. The advent of the cell phone had all but eliminated the need to leave messages on a recorder.

She pushed play:

> "Jennie, I got a job takin' a yacht to Malaysia. Pays good,
> but I gotta go right now. I'll be gone weeks. Don't like
> to do it, but it could work out good. I'll call when I can.
> Bye for now."

The message had been recorded from Mike at 3:10 p.m. A second message from Mike played after the tone:

> "Jen, I'm leavin' soon with Ronnie and Joel from the
> Royal Yacht Club. It's a motor yacht; name is *Getaway*.
> It'll be maybe ten days to get to Torres Strait, ten more
> to Malaysia. No satphone. I'll call when I can. Bye, bye."

The message was recorded ten minutes earlier, at 6:32 p.m.

Jennifer, disgusted and unhappy, sat down. There was a vibrancy to his voice she hadn't heard for weeks. She played the messages again. *Malaysia. Gone weeks.*

"Great," she said aloud and turned toward the kitchen, but then paused and began a replay of the last message again.

"Jen, I'm leavin' soon with Ronnie and Joel from the Royal Yacht Club. It's a motor yacht, name is *Getaway*..."

She stopped the message and turned on the desktop computer. Searching the Internet, she found the photo of the three men she had seen in the office and looked behind them in the picture to confirm the name of the yacht: *Getaway*.

"That's curious," she said softly to herself.

CHAPTER EIGHT

Mike expected an imminent departure from the yacht club after Ronnie and Joel arrived, but not until the Friday evening darkness settled in did Scott Wilson come aboard the vessel bringing with him his carry-on-bag, badly discolored facial welts, and extreme bitterness; he appeared to be upset and confused. Mike introduced himself and Ronnie and Joel before directing him to the master stateroom. Then he and his crew made preparations to get underway. Only then did Foster hand him the rest of the nine-thousand-dollar down payment before going ashore. Mike got a "clear out" from the harbor agent, cast off the lines, and the voyage was underway.

Jim Foster watched the yacht leave the harbor and then drove to downtown Sydney. He parked his car in the Grace Hotel basement garage, took an elevator to the ninth floor, and walked to a door that had "The Hospitality Suite" engraved on a rectangular copper plaque. He hesitated briefly and then rang the doorbell. From inside the room, Ray Dunn came to the door and looked through the peephole.

"Yep," he said, confirming the expected arrival of Foster to James Wilson, seated in a recliner with his back to the door.

Wilson signaled for Dunn to let Foster enter the room.

Ray Dunn was an advisor and confidant for Wilson. He had come to Australia from Sweden in his early twenties, for reasons rather unclear, and labored on the Sydney Harbour docks. At first, he worked as a collaborator and an operative for Wilson but later came to be his most trusted right-hand man. Fifty years old, he was medium height and weight with blonde hair and blue eyes. He was unmarried, and men had become his current romantic preference.

The large suite had tightly woven, light gray carpeting; the walls were painted white and the room was furnished with a red leather couch and two recliner chairs. The couch faced a large flat-screen television anchored to the wall above a long, three-foot-high, beige-colored bookcase. The recliners were placed on either side of the TV; a glass coffee table rested between them and in front of the couch. There were several other chairs and some table lamps. Behind the couch, in a separate room, was a kitchen and dining area.

A balcony overlooked downtown. Not visible to Foster was a bedroom containing a king-size bed, another flat-screen TV and en suite. Dunn sat on the couch. Foster walked past him into the room and stopped in front of the recliner across from Wilson. He remained standing while Wilson deliberately extinguished a cigarette, lit another one, and watched smoke from it curl upward toward the ceiling. Foster declined a cigarette offered to him.

"How'd it go?" Wilson questioned, without looking at him while taking yet another drag on his cigarette.

"No problems," Foster said, moving behind the chair.

"My son on board?" he probed, finally looking at Foster.

"Yeah, and two teenage crewmen."

"You want something to drink?" Wilson asked.

"No, I'm fine." Foster walked to the curtained window and looked out at the city lights.

"So Denham was the only guy you could find?" Wilson repeated a question he asked earlier in the day when Foster returned to get the down-payment money and the contract.

Foster suppressed a smile and answered while looking at a reflection of Wilson in the glass. "He's a damn good seaman and wants the money." Foster turned and faced him. "Ya couldn't a' done better on this short notice."

He knew it was only by chance anyone was available to take a yacht to Malaysia, or anywhere else, with only a half-day of preparation. Getting Denham was unexpected. "You're probably right." Wilson pulled a roll of bills from his pocket and gave him five hundred dollars.

Foster acknowledged his reward with a nod. Five hundred dollars was a paltry amount compared to the ten thousand dollars Denham received, but the risk was equal to the reward, and he didn't try to justify it any other way. At his age, he knew his limitations and exited the room with a brief thank-you.

Wilson and Dunn sat for a moment before Dunn spoke.

"I guess there was no one but Denham to do the job."

"You heard Foster," Wilson said, inhaling cigarette smoke. "He's a damn good seaman. Besides, it may work out better this way. With him out of the country, it'll be that much easier to find a way to pay him back for all his trouble."

"At least you got your boy on board," commented Dunn.

"Only because he loves his mother."

"Maybe so," Dunn said. "But the only reason he's still alive is because you're his father, isn't it? Still, I can't help wondering if he copped a plea it would have been okay."

Wilson shook his head no. "If the media learned he was in the house, they'd have dragged me into it. I don't need that kind of publicity now. This buys me time till after elections."

"And when they get to Malacca and there's no buyer?"

"I'll deal with that when the time comes." Wilson exhaled smoke. "Let's get out of here. I'll send a message to Charley if I want to see you."

———

October 5

Jennifer came into the office Saturday morning dressed in jeans; an olive green, high neck tank top; and running shoes.

Dennis was dressed similar to what he wore the day before.

He was surfing the web. Jennifer seemed to be in a bad mood.

"Have a bad night?" he asked.

"Mike's taking a yacht to Malaysia. There was a voice message from him when I got home last night."

"Wow, that's a long way," he declared. "Why leave a message; he could have called your cell?"

"Then he'd have to answer my questions," she said.

"Oh," he responded, with muted deference.

She turned on her computer and began her own web search.

"He said the name of the yacht was *Getaway*. Here, look at the picture I showed you yesterday." Dennis rolled his chair to her cubicle. "See the name on the yacht?"

He read the name. "*Getaway*. Mike's?"

"So the PM, Wilson, and Dowling are posing in front of this yacht and then Dowling dies and the next day my husband is taking it to Malaysia." She paused. "It bothers me."

"I'm not sure I follow; it's not even a recent photo."

"True, but somehow it seems interrelated. It would be interesting to know who owns that yacht," she wondered.

"Why would it matter?" he queried.

"Maybe it doesn't, but it's been troubling me ever since I got Mike's message," she stated. "I'm going to see if I can verify the registration of this one with ship registry."

"It's definitely a nice looking one," he commented.

"I can't help but think Wilson is involved," she remarked. "He's been on my radar since I was a political reporter."

"Can you be more specific?" he asked.

"Just a feeling, and it's not feminine intuition," she said. "I've heard about things he may have done in the past."

"Like what?" Dennis asked.

"He's a career politician with a law degree. He first made his mark with the law firm of Shanklin and Goetz, eventually becoming a partner. He's had seats on corporate boards and was an Opera House trustee."

"Sounds like a good resume," he remarked.

"He's the quintessential political operative," she replied. "He served in the State Parliament before gaining his Senate seat and only a few years later became Labor leader. He's survived several charges of corruption made by the Liberals, including claims his office got kickbacks on public contracts. Our paper and other print media initiated some provocative analysis, but nothing ever came of it. Today he's regarded as the most powerful man in Parliament. His personal life has suffered, though. A twenty-year marriage that produced one son ended in divorce ten years ago, and he never remarried."

CHAPTER NINE

Seven guests were seated at the table for another campaign dinner for Leonard Brown hosted by Margaret Farrow. They included David and Naomi Walters, Dr. Horace and Edith Tompkins, Thomas and Lois Nettleton, and Grace Ackerman. After enjoying a fine five-course meal, the talk had been subdued until after-dinner fruit cordials and soft cheeses were served. When someone brought up the topic of the previous dinner meeting, campaign advertising, the discussion abruptly changed.

"We're thinking of flooding the media with advertising instead of waiting until the last two weeks," Grace said.

"Wouldn't that seem to be desperate; do we even have enough resources to do that?" Mr. Nettleton asked.

"What about our contributions last month," said Mr. Walters. "Are we throwing good money after bad?"

"Beating a dead horse. That's what it's called at the track," Mr. Nettleton stated.

"It may just catch Wilson's campaign off guard," suggested Dr. Tompkins. "Maybe it's worth a try."

"The polls show us still trailing," Grace added. "The governor thinks an advertising blitz may be what's needed to boost his numbers."

"We've got to try something," the doctor responded.

"If the new ads haven't changed the polls, how can we be expected to give more money?" Mrs. Walters asked.

"That's right," continued her husband. "And what about the new production staff? I thought they were going to be the big difference-maker."

"There's only so much we can do with limited resources," offered Grace. "Historically, early campaign ads have been effective, and we feel there's a potential for some major gains."

"We understand, Grace," added Margaret. "I think we're inclined to go along with whatever the campaign suggests."

"And what about the fire last week, Grace?" asked Dr. Tompkins. "Will that affect the campaign?"

"Yes, what happened?" Mrs. Walters questioned.

"We don't know; the fire marshals haven't determined a cause yet," Grace answered. "Thankfully no one was hurt, but the annex is a total loss."

"Including the video library?" Mr. Nettleton inquired. "Won't that slow down your ad blitz?"

"We're filming new production shots at the Drama School. That's why Mr. Brown couldn't come tonight," she responded. "They should air on limited outlets by Tuesday, so by next weekend we'll be able to see how we're trending."

The diners began to squirm in their seats. Margaret asked her server to offer coffee and cake, but most of the guests stood up signaling they were ready to leave.

"Shall we meet again next Saturday night?" Margaret said. "That'll give us one more week to look at the poll numbers, and I'll serve something different that we can all enjoy."

"The lamb was superb, Margaret," offered Mrs. Nettleton.

"Next Saturday should be fine," said Mrs. Tompkins.

Grace approached Margaret as the others congregated at the door to wait on their cars. "We haven't heard from Scott since the other night, Ms. Farrow. Is he alright?"

"I don't know. He hasn't contacted me, either," she said.

"I was told he and Harriet were very close," Grace stated.

"I think they were going to announce their engagement soon," Margaret answered.

"Oh. Have you seen the papers..."

"It's absurd what they're writing," Margaret interjected. "Ray wasn't her companion. He met Harriet when she was with Scott, but it's improbable to think they were involved."

"Well, needless to say, our staff is in shock," added Grace.

"I hope I'll hear from him soon," Margaret stated.

"Me too. The dinner was excellent. See you."

"Thank you, Grace. Goodnight."

After the guests had gone, Margaret returned to the table for a cup of coffee. Like their previous meeting, she had not taken part in the after-dinner conversation. This time, besides thinking of Scott, she was recalling her relationship with Ray and the terrible tragedy that had left him and Harriet White dead. Ray had been a constant, dear friend and a great support. What about Scott? After the death of Harriet, she thought he would come to see her at the home in Balmoral.

Known as Adeline, the estate had been built forty-five years earlier by her parents Danforth and Adeline Farrow.

A celebrated Australian entrepreneur, her father expanded a small retail store into a chain of stores throughout Australia and New Zealand that made him rich. Her mother was a respected fashion designer and stylist. Adeline was the brainchild of her father, but her mother planned and oversaw its development, with an emphasis on the garden areas.

They had both died of cancer—her father thirty-two years earlier when she was enrolled at Macquarie. Her mother, from whom she inherited the estate, died two years ago. After her death, the estate sat idle for over a year.

Margaret recently financed an interior home restoration transforming the old rooms into a modern and spacious living area. The double high foyer with its vaulted ceiling entryway was left unchanged, except for new accessories. A visitor entering the home could turn right or left and walk toward a winding, open staircase that curved to meet at a second-floor landing overlooking a view of the living room bordered by a front room and parlor rooms on both sides. Walls that were not stone were painted in pastel colors;

large windows on the first and second floors provided a view of the harbor.

During the day the house could be flooded with natural light. A wide hallway to the left of the entrance led to a sitting room, theater, library, lounge, solarium, and patio. To the right was a lounge, den, billiard room, dining room, another lounge, kitchen, and pantry. There were six lavatories located throughout the downstairs.

Each of the five bedrooms upstairs had a bathroom, a walk-in closet, and dressing room. Also upstairs was a sitting room, small theater, reading room, and a separate washroom. The house had mostly hardwood floors with well-positioned area rugs. An elevator had been added to accommodate Margaret's disability.

After finishing her coffee, Margaret wheeled herself into an adjacent living room accompanied by Sandra who turned on a television airing a replay of a campaign rally in which James Wilson spoke about reforms he would pursue if elected.

"Turn that off, Sandra!"

"Of course. Sorry, Ms. Farrow."

CHAPTER TEN

t was late afternoon on October 5 and the fiberglass hull of *Getaway* cut through calm ocean water at sixteen knots, pushed along by her twin Deere engines humming in quiet synchronization. The yacht was US designed and built. Mike wouldn't try to compare her to some other luxury yachts he had piloted; she was a nice vessel in her own rite. Scanning the horizon on his seat at the flying bridge, he spied a cruise ship on the starboard side, no doubt going to the city they departed about forty-eight hours earlier. Since that time they had cruised north, northeast four hundred nautical miles into the Tasman Sea and would soon enter the Coral Sea, pass through the Torres Strait and then into the Banda and Java Seas bordering Indonesia, eventually reaching Malacca on the west coast of Malaysia. The itinerary would take two to three weeks to navigate assuming all went well, easily within the promised delivery date scheduled for mid-November, five weeks away. But Mike didn't want to think about the destination, or tomorrow for that matter. He was perfectly happy being in the present and on the ocean again.

God how he loved being on the sea. More than he loved his wife? He immediately pushed that thought aside and scanned the waters ahead for traffic. It was late afternoon. High cirrus clouds painted the sky.

He purposely began to visualize the decks of the yacht and picture in his mind the layout of each one, eager to avoid any further intrusive thoughts concerning his wife. He started by contemplating the bank of batteries in the engine room across from the two diesel engines driving the propellers. Above them, on an uncovered portion of the lower deck were two fishing chairs fastened to the floor. They were surrounded by cushioned bench seats hugging the rails and used as storage containers that held life vests, fishing equipment, and other miscellaneous items. Moving inside, two sliding glass doors opened into separate staterooms: the well-appointed master stateroom was spacious with plush carpeting, a king-size bed, wall-mounted fifty-inch screen television, chest of drawers, couch, table and chairs, closet, and bathroom. And a fine stateroom next to the master was decorated much the same, as its larger companion, but on a smaller scale.

A carpeted hallway near amidships separated two more twin staterooms from the others. They were handsomely decorated and fully furnished. Further forward, a room in the bow had mops, brooms, and storage containers and steps that provided access to the engine compartment.

Above the staterooms on the main deck, in order from stern to bow, was an outdoor lounge with a retractable awning, a large interior saloon, a galley, the utility room, and the pilothouse. The saloon had oak flooring and a bar extending half of its length; the walls and ceiling were all mirrored with frosted patterns, and there were bench seats and table and chair seating; two televisions were mounted on the wall above the bar; a theater screen could be pulled down for added viewing, but without a satellite dish no reception was accessible for any of the TVs. The galley, adjacent to the saloon, had plenty of shelf and counter space, a fully stocked refrigerator, double stainless steel sinks, a dishwasher, microwave, and stove. Forward the galley, a utility room contained a washing machine, basin, and a set of Bosch tools. Two Browning Model B25 pump-action shotguns were securely mounted on a wall rack.

The pilothouse, separated by a bulkhead from the utility room, featured a leather captain's chair at the helm in front of the control panel. The helmsman had an unobstructed view from this seat over the bow to the ocean through a panoramic windscreen. A companion chair was alongside, left of the helmsman. Both seats

     Ronald Lutz

could rotate three hundred and sixty degrees. A bench behind them spanned the width of the enclosure. Both the bench and the floor were carpeted with artificial turf. A walkway to the extreme left led to two bunks and a privy.

The upper deck was not enclosed. A dinghy was fastened at the rear above the saloon. Forward from the dinghy, an open space had been used for a satellite dish. Further forward was a multipurpose area. A table and several deck chairs, currently stowed, and another area covered by a fixed overhead canopy were ideal for open-air dining and relaxation. Further on above the pilothouse was the flying bridge, from where Mike was monitoring the path of the yacht. Reminded of the name of the yacht he thought of his voice message to Jennifer two days earlier. What he said was short and sweet. He was taking *Getaway* to Malaysia and would be gone for several weeks. He told her it would be ten days to the Torres Strait and another ten days to Malaysia, something like that, very matter-of-fact. And he had told her Ronnie and Joel were with him.

"He's still not eating," Joel said, interrupting the thoughts of Mike who turned and looked at him. He stood on the stairs connecting the main deck to the flying bridge.

"I gave him some more food," Joel continued, "but he just keeps saying he's not hungry."

Mike nodded his head in understanding. "I'll check on him when Ronnie comes up."

"I gave him some salve for his face too," Joel added.

As Joel returned below Mike smiled, gladly transferring his thoughts to his crew. Joel Jamison and Ronnie Wells had been with him for several years except when school interfered. Ronnie was nineteen, almost six feet tall, and was a blue-eyed blonde. His mother and sister, his only sibling, were killed in an auto accident when he was thirteen. His father never did recover from the loss and a few months later took his own life. After that Ronnie lived with his uncle but was in a new school with no friends. Then he met Joel on the school soccer team. They formed a bond, partly because

Joel lost his mother to cancer about the same time Ronnie's mother was killed. Joel was a year younger than Ronnie. He was five feet ten inches tall and had brown hair and brown eyes. He had no siblings.

Four years ago they stowed away on one of his boat tours. Running around together after school, both boys were seeking a job and soon made their way to the harbor area. Like Mike, they began to develop a desire to be on the sea and looked for a way to satisfy that yearning. Searching the waterfront and finding no work, they crept aboard the *Emerald Sea* tour boat. Mike was working as helmsman at the time and discovered them hiding in the storage hold. He offered to give them a chance to learn the boat operation, conditioned by a promise to stay in school. They soon were a regular part of the crew and were growing into men; both were slender but had muscular physiques. On the yacht, Ronnie was alternating with him at the helm. Joel had several duties: yacht engineer, steward, cook, and chief bottle washer.

The other passenger, Scott Wilson, was the son of the yacht owner, presumably onboard to ensure everything was working properly for the new buyer in Malacca. They were over forty-eight hours into the cruise and only Joel had seen him since he came on board, taking him food he didn't want and salve and ice he used to apply to his facial bruises.

The sun was low on the horizon, and Ronnie had taken over at the helm on the flying bridge as the yacht continued its smooth run over the sea. Mike finished up a sandwich and coffee in the saloon and then took the steps down to the lower deck and knocked on the door of the master stateroom. He waited a moment for a response and knocked again.

"Yeah," a washed-out voice came from within.

Mike opened the door and entered the stateroom. "You okay? Joel said you haven't eaten since you came on board."

Scott, seated on the edge of the large bed, looked rather bedraggled and forlorn. A tray holding food and water rested on a bedside table. With some effort, he raised his head to look at Mike.

          Ronald Lutz

"Where are we?"

"In the Tasman Sea, but we'll be enterin' the Coral Sea in a few hours."

"Where we headed?"

"Malaysia," Mike responded. "I thought you knew."

"That's quite a ways."

"Two, three weeks."

"So how long have you been operating this yacht for my father?" Scott asked.

"Never been on her before or met your father, far as I know," Mike replied.

"Who hired you?" Scott continued.

"You wouldn't know him. Look, I'm goin' topside to watch the sunset. How 'bout joinin' me? The earth keeps on turnin' so it's our last chance today."

Scott looked tentatively at Mike and then stood up and followed him to the top deck behind where Ronnie was seated at the flying bridge. Mike grabbed a deck chair for both himself and Scott so they could sit and admire the view.

"Never get tired a seein' that," Mike commented.

"I'm sorry, but I've forgotten your name," Scott said.

"Mike. Mike Denham. Joel's been bringin' you food, and that's Ronnie up there at the helm. They're a young crew but we've been together on different boats upwards a' four years, so don't be shy 'bout askin' them for anythin' you need."

"Young, but experienced," Scott added.

"You ever logged time on this yacht?" Mike inquired.

"No, I've never been on her."

"Well, the galley's always open. There's fishin' gear if you're so inclined. We've no schedules and we'll stay outta your way if that's what you want," Mike stated.

"Can I use my cell phone?" Scott asked.

"All we got is VHS."

"That figures," Scott remarked.

"There's a mount for a dish, but it wasn't here when I came aboard," Mike said.

"Guess I've no one to contact anyway," he said as the sun dropped below the horizon. "I think I'll try the food that..." He looked at Mike for help to remember the name.

"Joel," Mike reminded him.

"...Joel brought me." Scott got up and went below.

Mike joined Ronnie on the bridge.

"He finally came out," Ronnie said.

"Yeah, I was hopin' he didn't need Dramamine, not with these smooth seas, but it's not that. He's gonna be okay."

CHAPTER ELEVEN

— October 7 —

Bernie Carlson was standing in the break room of James Wilson's press office. He held a paper cup containing coffee purchased from a dispensing machine and was looking at the Monday morning print media releases from several newspaper and magazine publications. Thirty-eight years old and almost six feet tall, his black hair was already touched with gray and combed straight back. He had begun to show a middle-aged paunch but was smartly dressed in a Johnson tailored blue suit, white dress shirt by Calvin Klein, gray striped Gucci tie, and Jennen shoes. He looked to be the epitome of success and would be the first to tell you so, saying he was also proud of his wife, two teenage girls, and his home in the Sydney Hunter Hill neighborhood. Twelve years earlier he was hired to work in the office as a token gesture; his wife was the daughter of an influential senator. To his credit, he worked hard. Within three years he was promoted to press secretary, and with an unwavering resolve and Wilson's success in three ensuing re-election campaigns, had cemented his position.

He was an integral member of the Labor leader's team and, among other things, was responsible for placing positive news items for his employer in those types of publications he held in his hand. He nodded appreciatively at the first few articles he read, but then a scowl crossed his face as he came across a favorable clipping of Leonard Brown. He scowled again when he sipped the coffee.

Leaving the break room, Bernie nodded at Agnes Franklin, the office receptionist. He took a few more steps and caught one of his shoes on the pile carpeting, spilling half his cup of coffee. As he brushed the liquid off his pants, Jennifer walked in the front door holding a black carry-all tote. Attractive as ever, she stood almost five feet, seven inches tall, heightened by light green two-inch heels. Her dress was laurel green with a scoop neckline and hemline that was even with the knee, and a wide white belt drew attention to her hour-glass figure. Completing the look was shoulder-length blonde hair and hazel eyes accented with a soft gold eyeliner. Agnes greeted her, and Bernie stopped attending to the coffee spill in order to give the visitor a full-length inspection.

Jennifer wanted to find out if Bernie knew about the yacht in the Internet photo. She had already contacted ship registry, but they had a reputation of "slow to respond," and her patience was not what it should have been. Being bothered by the photo was probably unwise, but she couldn't help herself.

The press office was in an unremarkable building located on Francis Street not far from the *Daily Telegraph*. Jennifer had entered into a large open room furnished with several desks, armchairs, house plants, a television, and Agnes' desk.

"So this is where you hang out," she said to Bernie.

At the sound of her voice, he stopped his inspection, breaking into a happy grin when he recognized the reporter. "Jennifer! I don't remember you ever being here before."

"You're right—this is my first visit," she responded. "I tried to phone Friday night but could only get a recording."

"Let's go to my office," he said, ushering her along. He held out his cup for her to see. "Want some coffee?"

"No, thanks," she said, concealing her own scowl. They entered his office, and he took a seat at his desk. Jennifer sat in a chair across from him.

The pile gray carpeting Bernie had tripped on extended into his office. It was one of two rooms situated at that end of the building— the break room was at the other end—and it was nondescript. The desk had a credenza and next to it a two-drawer file cabinet. Two larger file cabinets at the back of the office bordered a small window with a view of the alley. Two other chairs and a plant made up the rest of the furnishings. The block walls were painted gray. A floor-to-ceiling window separated the office from the main room.

"I saw your editor at the Angel last week," Bernie said, referring to her boss and a local hotel bar. "Boy, was he in a grumpy mood."

"Jason?" she questioned, as he sipped his coffee.

Bernie smiled and nodded in the affirmative.

"I can see grumpy," she said. "Definitely not Happy or Bashful. But Dopey?..."

Bernie chuckled at her characterization, then said, "My staff should have told me about your message. For some reason, I didn't get it."

"I didn't leave one. I got the recording and hung up."

"Oh ..., okay. Well, what's up?" he asked.

"I wanted to get a statement or comment from Mr. Wilson about the death of Ray Dowling."

"We issued a statement to the news services late Friday," he said. "I'll tell my staff to email it to you."

"Thanks," she responded. "I must have missed it. I saw the one released by the PM."

"Mr. Wilson's statement is similar. He said Dowling had been a close friend or words to that effect," stated Bernie. "I'm sure you knew he was his chief of staff before Collier."

"Did he leave on good terms?"

"As far as I know," he answered. "He was probably ready for a change; he had that position longer than most," he said, and then sipped more coffee as she continued.

"I suppose you're right," she said. "But that's kind of a standard explanation, isn't it?"

Bernie ignored her comment. "I heard Dowling and the woman weren't married. And wasn't she black?"

Jennifer nodded yes, "Anything else on him you might know of, off the record if you like."

Bernie shook his head. "I hadn't seen him or heard from him since he finished his last contract. That's been four or five years or more," he said, and then sipped his coffee.

She changed the subject, and said, "Some polling data I've seen show Brown slightly ahead."

Her statement put Bernie's back up. "I haven't seen that. If anything Mr. Wilson is pulling away." Jennifer smiled, and he realized she was trying to rile him.

He looked at his watch. "Was there something else?"

She stood up to go. Bernie stood up also. "By the way," she asked, "do you know if Mr. Wilson has a motor yacht?"

"He owns a sailing yacht," Bernie replied. "I've been on it; it's a nice one. But a motor yacht? I don't know."

"I came across a photo on the Internet. It shows Dowling with Wilson and the prime minister in front of a yacht."

"Can you pull it up for me?" He backed away from his desk, inviting her to use his computer. Jennifer circled to his side of the room, all the while aware Bernie was undressing her with his eyes. She found the photo, and Bernie moved forward to look at it.

"I've never seen the yacht or the photo," he said.

"Nice looking, don't you think?" she stated.

"Dowling couldn't afford it. Have you checked with the PM?" he suggested. "Maybe whoever owns the yacht took the picture, or maybe they just used it as a backdrop."

"Maybe," she replied, picking up her tote. "Nice to see you, Bernie. Love what you've done with the office."

"Hey," he called to her. "What's that husband of yours up to these days? You know, if you ever get tired of being his second mate there are other fish in the water."

"Careful, Bernie. You're angling for some bad press."

He threw his empty cup at the wastebasket but missed.

⸻

Terry Godfrey was using a phonecard, purchased the day

before, to place a call on a public phone in the lobby of the Crest Hotel. Five feet, nine inches tall, his skin was fair and covered a pudgy, but not obese, frame. His Levi's, sneakers, and T-shirt were well-worn. His stubble beard was four days old.

A baseball cap with a team Scooters logo covered his unruly black hair. Twenty-seven years old, he grew up in the Sydney suburb of Canterbury and graduated from Temple High with a computer science major, promptly going to work for a local computer repair store. A self-identified geek, his aptitude for computer work soon attracted the attention of others, and he decided to do without higher education to pursue contractual engagements involving all things computing.

His first jobs were with homeowners and apartment communities but soon expanded to sole proprietorships and media agencies. It wasn't too long before his knowledge and expertise gained the attention of several suburban companies. Then big-name firms, realizing his talent, began offering him major financial contracts. When the elections were announced, Terry was sought by the Brown campaign for their technology department. He was hired to work under the supervision of Ray Dowling to transform an old annex building at the site of the Brown headquarters into a state-of-the art technological dynamo. The building became a center for production and design, computer research, and video editing projects.

Four nights earlier, the annex building had been destroyed by a now-confirmed firebomb. It was the same night Harriet White and Ray Dowling died. In a nervous state, and not just because of the fire, Terry dialed the number written on his hand. The telephone on the desk in the Denham home rang while Jennifer was opening a can of Meow Meal for Snoopy. She had been home an hour, long enough to have showered before changing into casual clothes. She had thought of going for a jog before her shower, but thinking about it and not doing anything was happening more and more lately. Tonight she had been in a thoughtful mood. The phone rang again. She put the cat food on the countertop and went to answer the phone.

"Hello."

"Jennifer Denham?" Terry asked.

"Yes."

"The newspaper reporter?"

"Who's calling?" she answered impatiently.

"I've got some information you may be interested in," Terry stated.

"Call me at my office," she said, about to hang up.

"It's about Marrickville," he stated hurriedly.

Returning the phone to her ear, "What about Marrickville?"

He blurted out, "I was there. I saw what happened—they were murdered."

"Well ...," she went on, skeptically, "have you called the police?"

"James Wilson was involved," Terry added.

"The Labor leader?" she asked, the tone of her voice betraying her interest. "Do you know him?"

"No, but the guy that shot them knew him."

She paused briefly to consider his accusation. "I'm not doing this on the phone," she said. "If you think you've got information I can use I'll meet you, but in a public place."

Terry hesitated briefly, then said "Okay, as long as I remain anonymous. No pictures."

"Do you know the Starbucks near the 'Rocks' on Alfred Street?" she asked.

"I can find it easy enough," he said.

"Can you meet me there, tomorrow morning at ten?"

"I guess so," he answered.

"Okay, how will I know you?" she asked.

He thought for a moment. "My T-shirt. It says, 'Think Geek.'"

"'Think Geek', she responded. "Okay. Well, let's see ...I can wear..."

"I know you," he interrupted. "Your picture's in the paper above your column."

"It's an old picture. My hair's longer now," she said.

Terry dismissed her remark. "I'll be there early. Come alone; no police and nobody else, or I don't come in." With that, he abruptly hung up. Jennifer remained at the desk pondering the call. She had picked that Starbucks because if it was a crank call and he didn't show up it was close to her office. Meanwhile, Snoopy had vaulted onto the kitchen island and was trying as best she could to have her evening meal right out of the can.

CHAPTER TWELVE

— October 8 —

Aboard the yacht, Scott was still struggling to deal with the events of the preceding week. He nibbled on the food Joel brought him and eventually got in the shower and shaved his beard. He even found some clothes that fit him in one of the closets. Cleaned up but still downhearted, he noticed his briefcase resting on the table next to the chair. It was the one with the SW embossment—the messenger briefcase bag. He forgot he had it with him. It had a zip closure with four interior compartments; an exterior pocket on one side had a snap closure, and there were two exterior pockets on the other side. Inside the case was a laptop, a CARE brochure, and some personal items. He sat on the recliner, pulled the bag to his lap, and opened it to an interior compartment and started to thumb through the partitions and examine the contents. He pulled out some papers before realizing they were marriage applications. Quickly shoving them back into the brief-case, he leaned back in the recliner and tried to think about what happened in the preceding week.

It had been six days since he returned from Jakarta last Thursday afternoon. Harriet had met him at the airport. He remembered how beautiful she looked. After visiting with his mother, they went on to Harriet's home in the late afternoon. His eyes began to tear up and he dropped the bag to the floor as he thought of her accepting the engagement ring. But his recollections turned horrific when he thought of Ray coming in and knocking him out. When he woke up, Harriet and Ray were dead, killed by the man with a scar. Tied up,

Ronald Lutz

he was hustled into the man's car, wondering why he hadn't been killed too. As soon as they crossed the Harbour Bridge, he knew they were going to his father's house. The imperturbable Scarface let him call an ambulance and then threw the phone in the bay. When the cobwebs in his brain began to dissolve that night, he was able to recall what had taken place. The man with the scar had said the home invasion was all about the DVD. That was the report to his father when they arrived: the DVD had been smashed. After his father and Scarface talked in private, his father gave him an account of what took place.

He said Ray was shot when he tried to wrestle the gun away from Scarface. Harriet was killed when she got in the way. Scott was not satisfied with the explanation. Aware his life might still be in danger, he nonetheless rebuked his father, pointing out the content of the DVD implicated both him and the prime minister in unethical and incriminating practices. Even if the disc was destroyed, he had watched it and could reveal what was on the video to anyone who would listen. He could announce its content publicly, assuring with certainty that, being his son, it would damage his father's campaign.

However, his father was prepared for just such a challenge and issued his own ultimatum in the form of a threat: leave the city or your mother might experience a fate similar to that of Harriet and Ray. After what had happened, and because of his past behavior, Scott knew his father wasn't bluffing, and so he agreed to board the yacht and stay on it until after elections. He didn't know what else to do. So here he was at sea while a reprehensible man in New South Wales was getting away with murder and about to win another election.

The cloudless sky was dark blue early Tuesday morning. It was 1:00 a.m. There was no wind; the air was warm and the sea calm as the yacht cruised along on autopilot with Mike manning the helm. Before taking over from Ronnie he looked to see that both the fuel and potable water were depleting normally and noted the twin six-cylinder engines were rotating along smoothly at eighteen knots, well below their maximum twenty-four-knot rating. *She's got average speed,* Mike had said when he first looked at her performance figures. To which Foster had replied, *Ya' won't need to go fast. She'll get ya' where yur goin' with the fuel ya' got on board.* Not profound, but sensibly accurate.

In those wee hours of the morning the clear southern sky was bright with stars overhead. A quarter moon had gone from view as Scott entered the pilothouse.

"Advance and be recognized," Mike said, kiddingly.

"So this is where you hang out. Everything going okay?"

"Smooth and steady," Mike replied.

"You sure couldn't ask for a better sea," Scott said. "How long you been at the wheel?"

"I switch with Ronnie every four to six hours."

"Does Joel take a turn?" Scott asked.

"Every so often, but he lost the coin flip. He's engineer and steward this trip."

"He's been checking on me, asking what I want to eat," Scott said. "He even gave me heat pads to put on my face, and witch hazel, I think."

"How'd you get messed up like that?" Mike asked.

"It's a long story," Scott answered.

"It's a long cruise," Mike responded.

"I'd rather not talk about it," Scott replied. "How about letting me take over?"

"Sure, if you're okay with it," Mike replied.

"I've operated my mother's yacht," Scott reassured him. "It's bigger than this."

"Okay, go ahead," he said. "Check the compass heading. The auto pilot's on; if you want to go manual hold the 'off' key for a couple seconds and you're on your own."

"Got it," Scott said. He kept it on autopilot and kept quiet for a minute before starting a new conversation.

"This yacht just plows through the water; it's an easy handle. How does she compare to others you've operated?"

"She's okay," he replied. "But the best ship I've been on was the Carnival *Spirit*. Eighty-eight thousand gross tons. She's been decommissioned."

"What did you do?" Scott asked as he scanned ahead.

"I worked up to staff captain."

"That's second in command, isn't it?" Scott questioned.

"Went Sydney to Auckland. Later Sydney to Singapore."

"You quit when she was decommissioned?" Scott asked.

"I quit 'cause my wife said I was gone all the time."

"Oh. That's understandable," Scott said. "But getting something with similar pay and grade must've been tough."

"What'd ya' say 'bout not wantin' to talk about it?"

"Oh, okay, gotcha," Scott said, focusing on the sea ahead.

Mike switched tacks. "What do ya' do when you're not cruisin' around?"

"I work with CARE Australia," Scott answered.

"The charitable outfit? What do you do with them?" Mike asked.

Scott responded, "Well, last week I was attending an international conference on hunger. The goal is to reduce global poverty and direct humanitarian aid to the needy."

"Hunger still that big a problem?" Mike asked him.

"It is. And more than we want to admit," Scott added.

"I 'spect so," Mike said.

Terry arrived early at Starbucks Tuesday morning and watched Jennifer as she entered. He waited fifteen minutes to make sure no one was with her and then waited five minutes in the beverage line to purchase a coffee Frappuccino before joining her at a back table. He was wearing a 'Think Geek' T-shirt, ball cap, Levi's, tennis shoes, and had put on sunglasses and false mutton-chop sideburns. She wore a beige pantsuit and dark brown one-inch heels and had consumed a cherry oat bar and most of a flat white espresso while waiting for him.

"Can I get your name?" Jennifer asked when he sat down.

He cocked his head to one side and showed a slight smirk.

"Well, how about a number where I can reach you," she went on, "in case I have more questions after we leave today." He recited a number that she added to her phone list.

"It's a message service," he said.

"Okay, so you said on the phone you know what happened at Marrickville, that James Wilson was involved."

"Yeah," Terry replied, taking a sip of his beverage, "but what happened there started at the Brown headquarters fire."

"The annex fire," she stated rhetorically.

"Ray had a video he said would end Wilson's campaign," he remarked. "Wilson found out and firebombed the annex."

"You knew Ray Dowling?" she asked.

"Yeah. Uh, I used to be his market analyst," he answered.

"Do you work in securities or the exchange?" she probed.

"I'm past that," he said, flashing a 'don't ask more' smile.

"Claiming the annex was firebombed may hold up," she went on. "But to say Wilson did it is a pretty strong charge."

"Your paper said torched. Isn't that the same thing as firebombed? And the guy that shot Ray and the woman all but told Scott that Wilson had it torched."

"Who's Scott?" she asked.

"Wilson's son. Ray told me about him. He volunteered for the Brown campaign and had the idea for the video."

"Wilson's son volunteered for the Brown campaign?"

Terry nodded yes, going on, "And he was at Marrickville."

At that statement, she closed her notepad as if to leave.

"Check with their campaign. He was a volunteer," he added, "but you'll have to take my word he was at the house."

She paused, then asked, "What was he doing there?"

"As far as I know, he and the woman were a couple."

"Why do you think Wilson's son would want to work for his father's opponent?" Jennifer asked.

"I think there was something personal between them. But really, it was because everything in the video was true."

"On the phone you said you were a witness. How did you happen to be there? Did anyone see you?" she queried.

"No one saw me. I followed Ray to the house. I phoned his home when I saw the fire. He didn't answer so I went to his place on the chance he was home. Sure enough, he just hadn't answered my call. When I told him about the fire he remarked it had to be because of the video, then as if he remembered, 'they gave Harriet a copy.' He got an address from his computer and ran to his car. It was obvious he was going to her place; he just left me standing there. I didn't see the address, so I trailed him on my scooter."

"You were following him," she urged him on as he paused.

"For about five kilometers before my bike stalled close to an intersection. But then I saw Ray's car in front of the house around the corner. So I pulled my bike onto the lawn."

"Did you notice any of the street names?" Jennifer asked.

He shook his head no unapologetically.

"Never mind," she said.

"It was a corner lot. His car was parked under a streetlight, so I left my bike near the edge of the road. A long yard sloped down from the house and a light was on over the back deck. As I started to walk toward the house, someone opened a door onto the deck. I decided to go that way; it was closer than going to the front of the house."

Terry took a deep breath before continuing with his account.

"I got there in time to see the guy shoot Ray and the woman. I didn't see him shoot her, but she was dead when I went to check on her later. Then he put his gun in Ray's hand and after that he broke up the DVD."

"Can you identify the man you say did the shooting?"

"No. He always had his back to me," he answered.

"Maybe recognize him in a lineup?" she prodded.

"All I know is he was tall, but no taller than that guy," he motioned toward a guy standing in the checkout line.

"Let's keep going," she said. "So you were able to see and hear everything from the deck?"

Terry picked up from there: "The door was open and when I got there Scott was on the floor. I thought he was dead but then he made a groaning sound. Then the guy shot them."

He paused to take another drink.

"After he shot them Scott got up. That's when the gunman told Scott the annex had burned and said his old man wanted him out of the house 'cause he didn't want any publicity. Take it to the bank, Wilson was behind all of it, the fire and the murders."

"So the annex was burned because of the video?"

"All the other copies must have been there," he stated.

"Do you know how the video was obtained?" she asked.

"Ray said Scott set up the equipment in his father's house. He got a fictitious order to install track lights."

"Wilson was being recorded secretly," she stated.

"Wilson had been accused in the past of corruption and ethics violations," Terry answered. "Scott thought he could get footage of him being candid in some of his discussions. They did. They used fiber optics to record him talking to the prime minister about several deals: illegal contracts with Iran, illegal immigrants, and contractor kickbacks. All that in one five minute session. Ray said they hit the jackpot. That was the video. But they were all destroyed in the fire and the guy broke up the one the woman had. He told Scott he was there to destroy her DVD. That's what he did; then they left."

"They?" Jennifer exclaimed.

"The guy forced Scott to go with him," Terry remarked.

"Was there only the one man with a gun?" she asked.

"He was the only guy there, except for Scott."

"Do you think he had a gun?" she asked.

"Scott? No, no way."

 Ronald Lutz

"If the shooter had the only gun, why shoot them?" she mulled. "He could have broken up the DVD and left. Instead, he made it to look like a murder-suicide."

"I don't know," he answered. "I never thought of it that way. But from what I saw he knew what he was doing."

"Do you know how the woman got the video?"

"No. Ray said she got it the day before," Terry replied.

"Then somebody had to tell the shooter she had it?"

Terry shook his head no. He didn't know.

"So you think the video was going to be a problem for the Wilson campaign?" she asked

"Yeah, Ray was clear about that," he said.

"Do you know where Scott is now?" she asked.

"No."

"You say he was forced to leave the home. Could he have been working with the shooter?"

"No," he answered. "The guy had to tie him up."

"You're sure Scott and the woman were a couple?"

"That's what Ray told me."

"If all you say is true, this man is still out there. Why not go to the police?" she said. "You could work with them to get the guy off the street."

"And have him find out I was a witness?"

"How could he?" she asked.

"He found out about the video."

"I wonder how he could have known," she reflected.

"I don't know," Terry stated.

"You said you saw the woman dead in the house. Could she have been dead before you got there?"

"I don't think so. Like you say, the guy had the only gun."

"Did you hear a shot from the bedroom?"

"No, ...but now that I think about it, all I heard when Ray was shot was a kind of muffled sound."

"How long were you in the house after they left?"

"Not long. I saw they were dead and got out."

"The ambulance got an anonymous call. Was that you?"

"No."

"Did you see the car they left in?"

"No. They went out the front; I was in back. And good for me. If my bike hadn't stalled I'd probably be dead too."

"One last thing: did you take anything from the house or take any pictures that would verify you were there."

"No."

"I still think you should go to the police. They can offer you protection," she suggested.

"For how long, one, two weeks? I'm not going into a witness protection program. I prefer staying anonymous."

"Okay, no police. Well, that's all I can think of for now. Unfortunately, the only way I'll be able to use your story in my paper is if I get someone to corroborate it."

"Great. Then this has been a big waste of time."

"If we could find Scott, that would help. Would anyone at the Brown campaign know how to reach him?" she asked.

He paused. "What makes you think I know anyone from the Brown campaign?" he stated, evasively. "I knew Ray, that's all. But you've got my story, for what it's worth."

They both stood up and prepared to leave.

Jennifer looked at him guardedly and said, "If you think of anything else call me at my office."

CHAPTER THIRTEEN

Almost six days after the murders on Pine Street the police had uncovered no new information. They talked with Wilson late Tuesday morning in the Grace Hotel suite, asking him about his son because his car had been seen frequently at the home of the crime scene. Wilson said they were not on good terms and had not spoken to one another for months.

After the police had gone, he went to bed with a woman who had been patiently waiting for him, the fifth woman in the same number of days. Dunn paid her cash when she left and then changed the TV from music on-demand to a local station.

"How long before the food gets here?" Wilson asked from the bedroom.

"I'll see if I can hurry them up," Dunn answered. He was about to call when the doorbell chimed. By the time Wilson finished dressing, his meal from the hotel kitchen was on a table set up for him on the balcony. When he was through eating he poured himself a second glass of wine and joined Dunn watching television and smiled at the antics of several contestants on a game show.

When it was interrupted by a commercial Dunn turned down the volume and Wilson lit a cigarette.

"Did the Jacks find out anything about your son?" Dunn asked.

"Some neighbor saw his car parked in front of the girl's house a few times, that's all."

"Was it there that night?" Dunn questioned.

"No, but it was there often enough the guy remembered."

"What ya' tell 'em?"

"We're estranged. Haven't seen him in a while."

"Did they buy it?"

"Why wouldn't they? It's true enough. I told 'em we hoped to resolve our differences one of these days. They were real nice about it. Said they'd stifle any negative talk so it wouldn't hurt my campaign. The cops can be real obliging sometimes," Wilson said. "You know, I think I'm going to increase my charitable donation to the Police Legacy Fund to show my appreciation for their good work."

"I think that'd be a fine gesture," Dunn responded. "We can use it in a campaign ad."

Dunn got some more drinks from the kitchen and came back to the couch just in time for another commercial.

The game show ended and the noontime news began with a story highlighting the relationship between Malaysia and Australia. It prompted a remark by Wilson.

"How long will it take them to get to Malaysia?"

Dunn muted the TV. "Three or four weeks."

"I want Denham taken care of as soon as they get there. It'll be the perfect opportunity to get rid of him when he's out of the country."

"It's been a long time since you put a hit on anyone. This will be the second time in less than a month," Dunn said.

"Sometimes it works out that way," Wilson answered and then lit another cigarette.

———

 center police headquarters. It was Tuesday afternoon. Earlier that morning she had met Terry, the supposed witness to the crime. She thought he gave a thorough explanation of what could have occurred and was fascinated with his having linked James Wilson to the shootings. However, his version contradicted the police conclusion of murder-suicide. Reluctant to see David Haggerty so soon after their meeting on the previous Friday, she still thought he

     Ronald Lutz

should hear the story the witness gave about Marrickville. Turning off the ignition, she stayed seated behind the wheel for a minute or so and used makeup remover to lighten the color of her cheeks. Sighing deeply, she got out of her car and went into the station and was ushered in to see Haggerty. He sat behind his desk, wearing a white shirt and blue tie; a gray suit coat hung over his chair.

"Is this business or pleasure?" he said, in the way of a greeting. "Or did you want another look at my new office?"

Handing him the crime scene video he had loaned her, she asked, "Have you learned any more about this case?"

"You really know how to sweet-talk a guy, don't you? I guess now I know why you were promoted to investigative reporting."

He looked down and spoke as if talking to the desk. "There's not that much more to learn." Raising his head up he looked at her again, and said, "We're sorting out some issues about the gun."

Jennifer arched her brow, questioningly turning her head.

"It wasn't registered to either victim and we haven't traced it to an owner, so it was probably stolen. Also, ballistics could not detect powder burns on the man's face."

"No powder burns. What does that mean?" she asked.

"A close range discharge tends to produce residue."

"So what do they think?" she probed.

"We don't know. Using a suppressor would explain it..."

"A silencer?" she interrupted.

"...It lessens the sound" he said. "Used with a handgun it can also lessen the recoil and that could eliminate any powder burns. It's been successfully tested. We've used it in court as evidence. In this case, a suppressor could have been used with the gun, but," he shrugged, "there wasn't any."

"I think I have a headline," she offered. "Police perplexed by muzzle puzzle."

"Very funny," he stated with a desultory tone. "Need I say this information is preliminary and not yet for publication."

"What you need is a witness," she suggested.

"Always a help," he said vacantly. "Do you have one?"

"Yes, but he doesn't trust police protection."

"Why would a witness need protection?" he asked.

"He says a guy murdered the couple and he's scared."

Haggerty, now more attentive, questioned her with a look.

"He called me last night. I met him this morning," she said. "He was on the back deck but couldn't see the shooter."

"The door to the deck was open," he conceded.

She added, "He saw the man shoot Dowling, then break the video disc. He also said James Wilson's son was there."

"Well, see, your witness spoiled it by trying to embellish—he went too far, introducing another person into the narrative, and we've already ruled that out. Someone could make up a good story about what happened by reading the tabloids. Even your paper had pictures of a broken disc."

"My witness said the disc implicated James Wilson, the Senate Labor leader. Maybe his son was there to get the disc."

"It's interesting your witness talks about that disc. A broken disc tells no tales, but it's a good way to keep the story going," he said. "As for Wilson's son, we're looking for him, but only because we want to ask him a few questions."

"So he was there," she exclaimed.

"Quite often. A neighbor told us his car was there a lot," Haggerty said. "But nothing shows he was there that night."

"A neighbor knew the car belonged to Wilson's son?"

"He wrote down the license number," Haggerty stated.

"That's one concerned neighbor," she remarked.

"We found the car at his apartment. The manager said it hasn't been moved for several weeks. We're still analyzing DNA and fingerprints we found in the home," he added. "If Wilson's son had been there we'll find out, but he's not a suspect. The main thing we want from him is to find out if he knows why Dowling wanted to kill the girl."

"My witness says Wilson's son was there," she protested. "And he says the woman and Wilson's son were a couple."

"We're here any time he wants to get in touch," he said. "Personally, I won't be holding my breath waiting for a call."

ACCORDING TO THE POLICE, SCOTT WILSON WAS NOT A SUSPECT in the Marrickville murders but was wanted for questioning. The witness Jennifer interviewed said he was at the crime scene. She decided to contact Margaret Farrow to ask about her son in hopes of locating his whereabouts. An appointment was set for the next day, and Jennifer arrived at the estate wearing light blue slacks, a beige top, and one-inch black pumps. Sandra Morse, shapely attired in gray slacks and a black short-sleeve top, met her at the door and led her to the library.

The room was painted white and light filtered in from several sources: a skylight, patio doors, and a glass-block wall. The carpet was white, close tufted, and covered the center of the room, exposing an oak hardwood floor around the perimeter. A large white fabric sofa, two round swivel chairs matching the sofa fabric, and two end tables were all positioned on the carpet surrounded by floor-to-ceiling bookcases set into the four walls. Each wall had a wheeled ladder to retrieve books from the upper shelves.

Jennifer was examining one of the books when Margaret entered in her wheelchair. She wore a black, chiffon dress.

"Hello, Jennifer. Do you mind my being so familiar?"

"Not at all."

"I read so many of your articles and the numerous columns you've written, I feel I know you personally," Margaret added.

"I'm flattered," Jennifer said.

"I hope our directions were accurate," Margaret said. "We were given a new address when we remodeled."

"They were fine. I've been to garden club meetings near here. I couldn't help noticing the wonderful gardens you have. And ...what an excellent collection of books."

"They've accumulated over a long period of time," Margaret said. "You're holding a first edition; quite a few have been signed by the author. But I suspect you're not here to talk about what's in my library."

Jennifer replaced the book and turned back to face Margaret. "Ms. Farrow, I know your son is Scott Wilson. I'm trying to find him. I wonder if you know where he is or how I can get in touch with him?"

"The police were here asking for him too. I'll tell you what I told them. I've not heard from him for a week now. He hasn't returned my calls. I don't know where he is."

"Is it unusual for you not to talk with him for as long as a week?" Jennifer asked.

"No, but considering what happened I expected a call."

Jennifer continued, "When did you last talk?"

"He drove here from the airport with Harriet the afternoon she died. Scott had just returned from Jakarta."

"Was ...Harriet in good spirits that day. Was there anything that might have foretold those later events?"

"No. She was her usual charming self. I can understand why Scott might have fallen in love with her. I think they were going to announce their engagement soon. It's hard to imagine what happened."

"The man who apparently killed her was your former husband's chief of staff at one time. Did you know him?"

"I knew Ray long before that," Margaret stated. "We met in college and were very good friends."

"Did you keep in touch with him after that?"

"We've always been friends. He was here last week."

"You must be even more bewildered by what happened."

"I'm sure there's more to the story than we know," Margaret said. "I don't believe Ray could have done what he's been accused of. He had a great curiosity about people and life. He left college to join AVI and go to Africa."

    Ronald Lutz

"AVI?" Jennifer questioned.

"Australian Volunteers International."

"Of course," Jennifer responded.

"While he was gone, I met Jim Wilson. I was seduced by his charm and we married. When Ray returned, Jim hired him to run his first campaign. Ray ran it for over twenty years."

"That's a long time in politics," Jennifer suggested.

"Well, they finally had a falling out several years ago."

"I'd love to know what caused that," Jennifer mused.

"I was partly responsible. I never hid my affection for Ray. Jim was always suspicious of him and became jealous. After the divorce, Ray eventually left his position with Jim."

"Many people consider James Wilson to be corrupt," Jennifer stated. "Are you in agreement with those thoughts?"

"I could tell you things. Proving them would be difficult."

"Maybe I can follow up with you about that some other time. Before I leave, I want to make sure you haven't thought of anything else since the police were here that could be at all related to the whereabouts of your son."

"It seems I get more and more forgetful every day but, no, I haven't. I pray to God I hear something soon. If I do I'll try and let you and the police know."

"Thank you for your time, Ms. Farrow."

When Jennifer got to her car she read a text sent to her from ship registry. It read:

Licensed owner of RCL140IQ5002: James Wilson.

Before leaving the Farrow estate, Jennifer looked to find the address of James Wilson on her cell phone. She found it was not far away in the suburb of East Killara and decided to drive there to see if he had been in contact with his son. As an excuse to see him she could use the information from ship registry and explain to him her husband was operating the yacht.

Upon arrival at his home, a doorman informed her Wilson was not available and not expected back in the near future. She gave the man her office number before leaving and, in turn, was provided with the downtown press office number. The contact person was none other than Bernie Carlson.

CHAPTER FOURTEEN

— October 10 —

By the time the yacht had motored through most of the Tasman Sea, all on board had settled into a regular routine. Scott made himself useful by occasionally taking a shift at the helm and helping Joel with chores. Several hours each day the engines were given a rest and a sea anchor deployed. They often took that opportunity to go for an ocean swim. One day, Scott got the fishing gear out and caught a grouper, which Joel served for dinner. They all agreed, after over six days on the ocean, it was the best meal of the voyage.

Thursday noon they entered the Coral Sea and continued on a fast pace toward the Torres Strait. They were well ahead of schedule, so Mike suggested they stop at Boigu Island, the northernmost populated island of Australia and, as far as he knew, still the home of former navy buddy Al Decker, who had been on the island operating excursion boats for tourists.

The island was only six kilometers from Papua New Guinea.

It was noontime and a couple of days from Boigu when Scott joined Mike in the galley.

"How goes it?" Mike asked.

"Okay. Can you believe the smooth seas we're having?"

"That's why I'm drinkin' coffee," Mike said. "I was noddin' off so Ronnie took over the helm."

Scott made a sandwich and joined Mike saying, "I don't think this sandwich will measure up to the grouper."

"Do us all a favor. Catch another one of those, will ya?"

"I'll see what I can do," Scott said smiling, then changed the subject. "What got you started as a yachtsman?"

"My ole man, and the navy," Mike replied.

"How was the navy?" Scott probed.

"It was okay," Mike said. "I was in three years"

"So from there you stayed on the sea operating yachts?"

"Quite a few," Mike answered. "I was ship captain of a superyacht for a time and other yachts. But I've worked on commercial vessels, cargo ships, a couple of Carnival cruise lines and charter boats. Last one was Sea Charter."

"Sea Charter. That sounds familiar," Scott said.

"They run tours outta Sydney Harbour near the 'Rocks.'"

"Maybe that's it. I've got an office on Circular Quay."

"Your office with CARE?" asked Mike.

"Yes. I interned with them when I was in college and they offered me a job after I graduated," Scott explained.

"Well, if ever ya' want another career you'll be ready cause a' the experience you're gettin' here," Mike offered.

"That's encouraging; right now my career is up in the air," Scott answered gloomily.

"You got plenty a' time to decide on somethin.'"

"The thing is, I thought I'd be getting married, but that's not happening."

"The gal take a powder?" Mike asked.

"Something like that," Scott said, nibbling on his food.

———

October 14

The Brown campaign donors were at the Farrow estate for yet another Saturday night dinner. The same people from the previous week were all in attendance, except Mrs. Nettleton. She was attending a food symposium.

Margaret and her household staff set another fine table. However, the night was so clear, she had the dining room patio doors opened and the table with all the tableware moved outside to a screened enclosure.

Instead of lamb, Margaret presented a main course of polenta crushed whole trout. Her menu also included stuffed deviled eggs and salmon rillettes with poached garlic soup, burgundy salad, and, to cleanse the palate before the main course, a light melon sorbet; alongside the trout was a cashew raisin rice pilaf; several different deserts were offered; the wine served with the trout was sauvignon blanc. Before and after dinner drinks ranged from ginger ale to scotch whiskey sans ice.

The conversation, like the week before, was very general at first. Compliments on the meal and the outdoor setting were given by all. Mr. Nettleton commented that his wife would be sorry not to have been there.

Asked whether she had heard from Scott, Margaret shook her head negatively. The women at the table voiced concern. They tried to encourage her with sympathetic statements like "Well, a young man his age has a lot on his mind," or "Spring is a busy time of year," suggesting those could be the reasons for his not communicating regularly. Margaret finally changed the subject, asking Grace if the new poll numbers were out. With that suggestion, she passed around some informational printouts.

"What do we have here?" asked Mr. Nettleton.

"It's the newest polling numbers," Grace said. "As you can see they're improving."

"According to the *Daily Telegraph*, Wilson has a bigger edge than he had last week," warned Dr. Tompkins.

"I saw that too," said Mr. Walters.

"The *Telegraph* has endorsed Wilson," Grace cautioned. "We expected those numbers from them. But Nielsen and Newspoll are neutral. They show our support has increased."

"Maybe," said Dr. Tompkins, "but we still trail in both polls."

"Personally, I'd like to meet with Leonard again," said Mr. Nettleton, "just to get a feel for his frame of mind."

"I think that's a good idea," declared Mrs. Tompkins.

"I can always reschedule my weekdays," Margaret said.

"Well, we can set up something," Grace suggested, "but it might be better for those who want to see him to meet at the same time. If you tell me your schedules, I'll coordinate it by email."

"Good," said Mrs. Walters. "Can we use Facebook?"

"The Busby's don't use Facebook or Twitter," said Grace.

"But if we're going to do it that way," said Dr. Tompkins, "maybe we should skip meeting in the future. If we use email some of us might find it easier to say what's really on our mind."

"If you ask me it will take some kind of major revelation, or something shocking, to turn this race around, like a secret or missing tape," Mr. Nettleton proclaimed. "Something like what happened in the Watergate scandal they had in the US back in the '70s."

 Ronald Lutz

CHAPTER FIFTEEN

— October 15 —

The Sunday morning temperature on the Island of Boigu was already quite warm when *Getaway* dropped her anchor near Boigu village. The harborage was applauded by the men, even though no one on board had heard of the place except Mike. After sixteen hundred nautical miles—eleven ocean days—there was a great desire to recover their land legs. With an area of ninety square kilometers and its highest elevation less than eighteen meters, the island was ideal for just such an exercise. Raising goats and fish farming were major occupations of the few hundred inhabitants, but the leisure activities of tourism and recreation provided most of the commerce and were what enticed Al Decker to settle on the island. He and Mike kept in touch, off and on, over the years. A loner and an adventurer, Al had never married but found a place to call home on Boigu. He bought two excursion boats from a Papua New Guinea dealer and, after restoring them, started a charter excursion company that hired out the boats for tours.

Five years ago, convinced he had found his idyllic niche on Boigu, he invited Mike to fly up and inspect his operation. Mike was pleasantly surprised by what he saw. By this time Al had four boats and employed a workforce that took care of everything from maintenance to scheduling to ticket sales and conducting tours. He lived in a hut befitting his lifestyle.

Trying to remember the location and appearance of the bungalow, Mike set out with Scott to find a small wood frame home painted white with blue trim. An open cement porch six-meters wide, the width of the hut, and two-meters deep spanned the front, and three planks in the middle served as entrance steps. A thatched roof over the porch was supported by end posts and poles on each side of the steps, and a center door opened into the living room, also the width of the hut, from the porch. A hall on one side of the hut extended about nine meters, past a kitchen and pantry, two bedrooms, and a utility closet and lavatory. A window air-conditioner unit and ceiling fans circulated the air; no furnace or heating equipment was required in the tropical climate. Most of the furniture was cushioned rattan.

Seen from inside, streams of sunlight filtered through the thatched roof and spread over the bungalow porch floor as if greeting the woman whose silhouette appeared in the front doorway. She admired the view of the ocean before going out. In her mid-thirties, she stood five feet, two inches tall in her bare feet with eyes of blue and cropped auburn hair that had blonde highlights; she presented a sultry, sensual look, dressed in white linen shorts and a tank top. Stretching her arms up a few times before touching her toes, she then sat in one of the wicker chairs on the porch and reclined comfortably while continuing to look at the view. Closing her eyes for only a few moments, she opened them to see Mike and Scott, both wearing shorts and tank-top shirts, standing next to the steps.

"Can I help you?" she asked getting up from the chair.

"We're looking for Al Decker," Mike answered.

"He's in the village. He'll be back any minute," she said.

"Anywhere in particular?" Mike asked.

"He's getting groceries." Her initial surprise at seeing the two of them had passed. "You can wait if you like," and she motioned for them to sit down, curious about these strangers.

Mike was curious, too, as they all took a chair.

"Hope we didn't startle you out of a nap," he said.

"Not at all. I was just resting my eyes," she stated. "Is Al expecting you?"

"We've run a yacht up from Sydney," he said and flashed a smile. "My name's Mike Denham."

     Ronald Lutz

"Katherine Decker," she said, returning his smile. She looked at Scott.

"Scott Wilson," he said with a tepid grin, adding, "Our cell phones won't connect. Is there any service here?"

"No, I can't use mine either," she said. "Al has a landline if you need to make a call."

"Well, if you think it's okay. I'll be glad to pay him."

"The phone is to the right as you go in the house."

Scott accepted the offer and went into the bungalow.

"How do you know Al?" she asked Mike.

"We were in the navy together," he replied, "but I haven't seen him for several years. Didn't know he got married."

"I'm his sister. I'm visiting for a few days from Hong Kong. I hadn't seen him for quite a while either."

"Didn't know he had a sister," Mike stated with a hint more interest in his voice. "How long you stayin'?"

"Well, I had planned two weeks. Don't tell Al, but I've been here five days and I'm ready to move on," she said.

"Back to Hong Kong?" Mike asked.

"I'm on a four-week holiday. From here I go to Bali."

"Ever been there?" Mike asked.

"No, have you?"

"Not long enough for it to count," he said. "You bein' on holiday must mean you're a workin' girl."

"It's been a long time since someone referred to me as a girl," she said smiling. "I'm the property manager for a real estate firm."

"Strikes me you might a' been one a' them runway walkers if you were taller."

"That's very nice of you to say," she said, looking at him with a renewed interest of her own. "And how long will you be staying?"

"A couple days," Mike said as Scott rejoined them. "We're goin' to Malaysia to sell the yacht."

"That's a long trip. First to here, then Malaysia."

"Long, but pleasant so far," Scott suggested.

"What happens after you sell the yacht?" she asked Mike.

"Back to Sydney, unless somethin' else comes up."

She turned to Scott. "Were you able to get through?"

"Yes, I left a message," he answered, then to Mike, "Maybe we should look for your friend in the village?"

"I hope you won't run off and miss him," she stated.

"We've got plenty of time," Mike said.

"Did anyone else come with you?" she asked.

"There's two crewmen—teenagers," Mike stated. "You can see the yacht from the road," Scott added.

"Will you pass Bali on your way to Malaysia?" she asked facetiously, eager to leave.

Mike looked at her and then glanced toward Scott. Before he could reply, she suddenly stood up to greet Al, returning from the village, carrying a grocery bag and newspaper. He also wore shorts and a T-shirt and was about the same build as Mike with brown hair and brown eyes; he had a generous display of tattoos on both arms and other parts of his body.

His quizzical expression when first seeing the visitors changed to a broad smile when he recognized Mike. They exchanged a navy hug and shook hands, and then Scott was introduced. The men sat down and the navy men began to catch up on what they'd been doing. Katherine took the groceries inside and returned with drinks and snacks. She excused herself to change clothes and came back to the porch wearing a tropical outfit, a layered mini dress with a berry-colored outer skirt and white slip, white sandals, and a wide-brimmed straw hat. She sat and listened for a while to her brother and Mike talk about their recent exploits.

As the two friends continued to reminisce, Katherine asked Scott if he would walk with her to the harbor so she could see the yacht. On the way, he had little to say, but she talked about her stay on the island and her looking forward to continuing on to Bali. She noted that their arrival was not only a surprise but a welcome change, saying there was little entertainment on Boigu. As they rode the dinghy to

       Ronald Lutz

the yacht, anchored a short distance from the dock, several local curiosity seekers were making their own inspection from the waterfront.

Katherine was impressed even before she climbed the steps to go onboard. Ronnie and Joel, excited to have an attractive woman on board, gave her the deluxe tour, including a peek at the engine compartment. Later, while Ronnie explained the controls in the pilothouse, Joel set out a table and chairs underneath the top deck canopy and served drinks. She was even more impressed after seeing the layout and thought to herself how wonderful it would be to leave Boigu on a yacht.

When they returned to the bungalow, Scott tried to call his mother only to get her voice mail again. While Mike and Al talked on, Katherine walked to the beach.

———

Jennifer was typing on the home computer when her cell phone rang. She was relieved to hear Mike's voice.

"Hi, Jen. Hear me okay?"

"Yes. Are you alright?"

"I'm okay. Get my messages?" he asked.

"A week ago," she said indignantly. "Where are you?"

"Boigu. Stopped to see Al Decker."

"Who's Al Decker?"

"A friend from my navy days. I've mentioned him before; I'm usin' his phone. How ya' doin'?"

"Fine. How are you and the boys?"

"We're good. Jen, I'm wiring you ten thousand dollars tomorrow. It's the advance I got for this trip."

"A nice round figure," she said. "Will there be more?"

"A hundred thousand, when I get to Malaysia."

"So that's why you passed on the harbor master job."

"Too much to turn down for a few weeks cruise."

"In one of your messages you said the yacht is called *Getaway*," she stated.

"Yeah. She's a nice one."

"Ship registry says James Wilson owns it," she posed.

"You checkin' up on me, goin' to ship registry?"

"Is anyone else with you besides Ronnie and Joel?"

"The owner's son."

"Scott Wilson?" she asked.

"Is he in the ship registry too?" he asked tersely.

"No. Listen, Mike," she cautioned, "he was involved with a woman who was killed—about the time you left Sydney."

"He mentioned a woman," Mike said.

"A man was killed too," she explained. "The police wanted to talk to him after it happened, but he left with you."

"You thinkin' he had somethin' to do with it?"

"Satisfy my curiosity, won't you?"

"I'll see what I can find out. We'll be leavin' here soon, so it'll be a while before I call agin. And I better go 'cause I don't want to run up Al's bill. He won't let me pay it."

"Mike, I miss you darling. I love you—be careful."

"Remember you got some money comin'. Bye, baby," he said as he hung up the phone.

Katherine suggested they all dine at the island restaurant that evening. They all agreed, and then Mike and Scott walked to the harbor with Al to show him the yacht. They remained on board to change clothes, and Al returned to the bungalow. Katherine met him, eager to discuss her idea she thought of on the beach: to go with the men on the yacht when it departed.

Al protested, saying they had been together only a few days after being apart for five years. He argued her flight, booked for the following week, would get her to Bali faster than if she took the yacht. But she had made up her mind, explaining to him that, truthfully, as much as she enjoyed his company and generosity, she was bored. Going to Bali on the ocean seemed very appealing; she had never been on a yacht and it would be fun. She promised to stay in touch and said she might make a return trip in a couple of

    Ronald Lutz

years for another visit. Seeing she would not change her mind, he advised her to discuss the idea with Mike before canceling her flight.

She returned to her room and began to pack but decided to rest until dinnertime. Removing her clothing, she stretched out on the bed and covered herself with a sheer negligee. She set a clock alarm for seven—they were dining at eight—and then took a small green tin from the bed table and removed a hand-rolled joint. It would be the first one she smoked since coming to Boigu. Was it because of the rather contentious discussion she had with Al, the excitement of a possible ocean voyage, or the attractive appeal of Mike Denham?

She lit the cigarette and inhaled slowly to neutralize an initial rush, then rolled on her back and stared at the ceiling fan rotating slowly overhead. Inhaling a second time, she turned to look at her luggage along the wall. A smile formed on her lips. After inhaling again, her mind began to relax. She extinguished the joint and fell asleep.

———

A GECKO LIZARD SCAMPERED ON THE WALL OF THE RESTAURANT lounge and paused to watch Al, Katherine, Scott, and Mike take a seat at a coffee table. The four acquaintances wanted to relax and have an after-dinner drink. The small diner was not fancy, furnished with folding tables and chairs and an old oak bar. The lounge had couches and chairs placed around several coffee tables, and even though the room had electric lighting, candles were used after nightfall for the most part. None of the windows had glass, but they all had adjustable screens and shutters. Solar lights staked near the beach illuminated the ocean surf and offered a pleasant view.

It was almost 28°C. The men all wore casual shorts and tropical shirts. Katherine had on peach-colored shorts with a mint-green top. At first, the talk was about their dinner and life on Boigu. Then Katherine lit a cigarette and changed the conversation, just as the gecko charged after a lowly cricket.

"It's too bad Ronnie and Joel couldn't join us," she stated. "It was Ronnie's turn to stay on board," Mike said. "Joel's keepin' him company. They can eat here before we leave."

"When will that be?" she asked.

"I want to go with Al on one of his excursions," Mike said. Looking at Al, he suggested a date. "Tomorrow?" Al nodded in the affirmative. "Then we'll leave on Tuesday if that's alright with Scott and our crew."

"Okay by me," Scott replied.

"I was half kidding this morning," Katherine inquired of Mike, "but I wonder …could you be persuaded to take me with you? On the map, it looks like you go past Bali to get to Malaysia. If you do, would it be too much out of your way to drop me off? My flight isn't scheduled to leave here for another ten days."

"Well, it'll take that long for us to get as far as Bali," Mike stated. "You won't lose any time by taking your flight."

"That's what I told her," Al commented.

"Even if it took longer, it would be worth it," she replied. "I've never been on a yacht; it would be an adventure. I'll gladly pay my way."

"You might be crowded by four men," Scott suggested.

"From what I saw, you had a lot of room," she said, "but I don't want to take someone's space and rock the boat."

"Rock the boat," Mike smiled, "I like that."

"I can travel light," then turned to Al and said, "Can you send my large bag home if I arrange it?"

"I haven't heard them agree yet," Al cautioned.

Mike looked at Scott. Scott shrugged his shoulders as if to say it's your decision.

"Well, what do you think?" she asked, looking at Mike.

Mike looked back at her. "Appears we're goin' to Bali."

"For real!" she exclaimed. "You wouldn't kid me, would you? It is on the way, isn't it? You'd have to go close, wouldn't you?"

Mike smiled. "Like you say, it's on the way. We might have

stopped there anyway. I'll just need to get entry forms to fill out, but that's nothin'. Scott, we'll put her in the master stateroom. She'll have enough room, even for her large bag, and you can move next door."

"Where will the boys sleep?" she asked.

"They usually bunk behind the pilothouse. You bein' onboard won't bother them."

"You sure they won't mind?"

"Are you kiddin'. Having an attractive girl ...woman on board. They'll love it."

Scott whispered in Mike's ear, "Why do I get the feeling you'll be loving it too?"

The conversation ended and they all got up to leave. The men followed her outside. They had enjoyed the dinner and talk and all left with a feeling of satisfaction, somewhat like the sensation the gecko experienced as he chomped on the cricket.

Jennifer decided to call Margaret after she talked with Mike to tell her Scott was okay. If he hadn't already called her she was sure it would put her mind at ease. She was able to get a cell phone connection on the first try.

"Hello, Jennifer," Margaret answered her greeting.

"I wanted to ask if you've heard from Scott?"

"No, but I think he tried to leave a message. I have a new phone and deleted at least one message by mistake."

"He's on Boigu Island," Jennifer said.

"Boigu, near New Guinea? Is he alright; what's he doing there?" Margaret asked.

"He's fine. My husband is taking a yacht to Malaysia. He called me earlier today. He said your son is with him. They stopped at Boigu."

"Your husband operates a yacht? How did he meet Scott? Does it have anything to do with what happened to Harriet?"

"I'm sure it does, but I don't know yet. My husband is piloting a yacht for the owner and met Scott by chance."

"You say he's going to Malaysia?"

"Yes."

"I wish I could have got his message."

"I hope you won't be anxious about him," Jennifer said. "I'm sure he'll try to call again. You can be certain as long as he's with my husband your son is in good hands."

"I appreciate that. I've been praying for the Lord to keep him in *His* hands."

"I understand."

"Scripture says 'do not be anxious about anything, but in everything, by prayer and petition, with thanksgiving, present your requests to God'..."

"That's a wonderful sentiment," Jennifer remarked.

"...it goes on: 'and the peace of God, which transcends all understanding, will guard your hearts and your minds in Christ Jesus.'"

"You may cause me to look at the Bible again."

"It's a source of comfort for me," Margaret stated.

"I'm sure. Hopefully, you will hear from Scott soon. If I get any more information, I'll be in touch. Goodbye for now."

"Thank you so much, Jennifer. Goodbye."

CHAPTER SIXTEEN

— October 21 —

Four days after departing Boigu Island, the yacht continued along on its journey through the Arafura Sea, between Papua New Guinea and East Timor, Indonesia, and was soon to enter the Banda Sea. The weather was fair and the mid-morning temperature was 30°C. From the starboard side walkway Scott watched the interplay inside the pilothouse between Mike and Katherine. If ever he saw a woman openly flirting, it was happening right before his eyes in real-time. She was barefoot and wore tight blue short shorts with a sheer white midriff top. Mike was bare-chested and was wearing only cargo shorts and boat shoes. They both seemed to belie their age by the way they were carrying on; they were getting along famously. Katherine was the aggressor, while Mike played the willing victim and offered no resistance. Their interaction reminded Scott of the chemistry he and Harriet experienced when they were together. It had been eighteen days since she had been murdered in the home she rented in the Sydney suburb of Marrickville.

A light breeze began to spring up and swiftly turned to the east. The seas began to churn as the prevailing westerly wind shifted 180 degrees and storm clouds began forming behind them. The sudden change got the attention of Scott, and he looked back at the bridge. Mike noticed the different conditions, too, and had taken the wheel from Katherine. She joined Scott on the walkway, her flirtatious advances having been terminated by the weather.

"He says the wind is freshening," she said.

"This is the first choppy seas we've had," Scott remarked.

They both were looking toward ominous skies but at the same time enjoyed the brisk breeze, and the occasional spritz of water cooled them off even more. Then the yacht lurched slightly and wave spray drenched them both. They gasped in surprise and shock. Scott laughed for the first time in over two weeks. Katherine laughed, too, but then realized the spray had caused her top to become transparent. It was clinging to her body and made it look as though she had nothing on from the waist up. Scott took notice of her situation and tried hard not to stare—without success.

"Watch the spray," Mike said, also staring with approval from his perch in the pilothouse.

"Is he kidding?" she said, stomping off to change clothes.

Next morning, the sun was barely visible on the horizon when Scott made his way to the pilothouse. Mike was at the helm listening to weather reports on VHS radio and trying to stay alert. Seeing him stifle a yawn, Scott offered to take the helm and Mike didn't argue. He reminded him the yacht was on autopilot, to check the compass and watch the AIS traffic signal on the monitor.

"So you think I'd make it as a helmsman," Scott remarked.

"Like I've said, a backup for your other job," Mike joked.

"I won't think about that till elections are over," he replied.

Mike snorted. "What's that got to do with it?"

"I didn't say anything before," Scott explained, "because I thought you might be working for my father, but I'm here because he ordered me to leave the country till elections are over."

"Aren't you past havin' to obey your ole man?" Mike asked.

"It's more complicated than that. I think he ordered my fiancée killed," he explained. "She was African American. I think he believed our relationship would hurt him politically."

Mike said, "I called my wife on Boigu. She's a reporter in Sydney. She'd fig'urd out you were with me. Said a woman and man were killed the night before we began the cruise. The police are lookin' for you as bein' connected to it somehow."

"You might have told me," Scott said. "What else did she say?"

     Ronald Lutz

"She wanted to find out what you knew," Mike stated.

"Nothing really," Scott replied. "The woman killed was my fiancée, Harriet White. I gave her an engagement ring the night she was murdered. The man that was killed was Ray Dowling. If your wife is good enough to track me here, she probably knows everything else I could tell her."

"She was curious about who owned this yacht."

"She better be careful. If my father finds out she's nosing around, well …she better be careful, that's all," Scott added.

"Your father must be incredibly desperate or incredibly insecure."

"He wouldn't admit to that. But I'll tell you, if he feels endangered, he'll use any means, lawful or not, to extinguish what he views as a potential threat. That's why I haven't seen him for years until I agreed to this cruise."

"Why not go to the police?" Mike asked. "If he's tryin' to intimidate you, aren't you tellin' him he can get away with all he's done by you leavin' the country?"

"The thing is, he didn't threaten me, he threatened to kill my mother. That's why I agreed to come on this cruise."

Mike listened as Scott recounted what happened prior to his coming aboard the yacht. He told how he opposed his father's campaign and signed on to work as a volunteer for Leonard Brown. He explained how the video was secretly obtained using a hidden recording device set up in his father's den. The recorded footage showed the prime minister talking with his father about their complicity in corrupt government schemes. He felt the distribution of the video would have ended both their campaigns for reelection. Harriet had been given a copy. They watched it the day he got back from Jakarta. Then Ray Dowling unexpectedly came to the house to get the video and in the process knocked him out. He woke up to find both Harriet and Dowling dead, killed by a man hired by his father. He wondered, if not for the unwanted publicity, he may have been killed too.

His father told him Ray died in a struggle to get the video disc and Harriet was killed inadvertently. He called her death collateral damage and said the video disc had been destroyed. After that came the ultimatum: go on the yacht and stay away until after the elections or his mother would be killed. So he came aboard the yacht. There didn't seem to be an alternative.

"Can't say I blame ya' for not getting along with your ole man," Mike said. "I've experienced rough goin's on around the docks, but what you're sayin' is worse than that."

"As far as I know, the video's never been released. If it had been, father could not threaten my mother or me."

"No way to protect your mother?" Mike asked.

"I didn't think I could risk it. Her home is in a walled estate, but it's no safeguard when you get right down to it."

"You best be watchin' for your ole man when you get back," Mike said. "Once elections are over, he won't be worryin' 'bout bad press when it comes to dealin' with you."

"You're probably right," Scott replied.

"How long did ya' know Harriet?" Mike asked.

"We dated almost two years. She was from California but was studying as an international student in Sydney."

"That's tough. Strange the way you said your old man described her death as being collateral damage."

"Father had been spying on her; he knew we were dating. He said it on the video. I think he didn't want to deal with an interracial couple. To him, we were bad publicity."

Then he told Mike about his mother, but not that she was independently wealthy or that he was destined to be the heir to her fortune. But Mike already knew his mother was wealthy. After all, she owned a yacht and lived in a walled estate.

"I'm gonna rest my eyes," Mike said, stifling a yawn. "Give me a few minutes before you go below."

He slept on the bench in a sitting position for forty minutes. When he woke up, Scott gave him a wry smile.

 Ronald Lutz

"I suppose a few minutes could be interpreted as forty."

"Guess my watch stopped," Mike said, sheepishly.

———

Smooth seas returned the next morning but now the air was very humid; the full impact of the storm had been far to their east. Wearing cutoffs and a striped top, Katherine was on a bench seat in the saloon holding a cup of tea and gazing out the window. Scott, wearing only khaki shorts, came up the steps from below and saw her looking out over the ocean.

"Morning. No more choppy seas," he said.

"I'm so glad," she replied, turning to greet him. "There's coffee brewing in the galley."

"That's what I'm here for." He got coffee and returned, sitting across from her on the bench on the opposite side of the saloon. "Joel makes good coffee," he said after taking a sip.

"Don't tell anyone, but I made it this morning."

"Tastes every bit as good as his," he noted after taking another taste. "Thank you very much."

"Just between the two of us, Joel's is much better."

He smiled. "I hope you'll excuse my being standoffish. Sometimes it takes a while for me to adjust to people."

She returned his smile, "I'm kind of like that too."

"Seems we'd see more of each other," he stated.

"You'd see me if you helped with meals and cleanup," she said, pretending an attitude.

"Ouch! Maybe I'll go back to being standoffish."

There was a quiet pause as they both drank from their cups.

"Have you been able to sleep?" he asked.

"Off and on," she replied. "I had to smoke a joint last night, but I've only done that once so far."

"Yeah, I figured as much; it's hard to disguise that aroma."

Mike came down the steps into the galley, poured himself a cup of coffee, and got a biscuit. He walked into the saloon and held his coffee cup up high.

"Joel didn't make any topside," he remarked.

Sensing an update, they waited for him to go on, but he took a bite of the biscuit first.

"We're more'n halfway," he said, after sipping the coffee.

"So, another three or four days?" she asked.

"'Bout that."

"Will I be able to call ahead to confirm my reservation?"

"Sure," Mike said. "I'll be callin' for a docking berth too."

   Ronald Lutz

CHAPTER SEVENTEEN

— October 27 —

Bali's Benoa Bay Harbour was a comfortably warm 26°C at mid-morning as Mike guided *Getaway* into the crowded marina. Ronnie and Joel hoisted arrival flags on the prow and looked for the docking berth Mike had reserved the day before on the radio call. Katherine and Scott were also on deck. She had been able to confirm her Hyatt reservation at the same time Mike called for a berth.

The men wore shorts, T-shirts, and tennis shoes; Katherine had on a gray skort, sheer white top, and sandals. She was taking pictures of everyone with a digital camera and got a few shots of the *Sun Princess* cruise ship docked on the other side of the harbor. Before long, Ronnie gave a shout, pointed to a berth at the end of a long pier, and soon the yacht was securely docked. They first went to a customs official to report their arrival and have him stamp their passports and check the yacht. A departure date was set for November 1. Then they all purchased temporary SIM cards for their phones at a kiosk near the head of the pier. After those activities, they all went ashore except for Mike.

The harbor was midway between the Grand Hyatt Bali resort and the city of Denpasar, twelve kilometers distant each way. Parked at the head of the pier were several taxis, one of which transported Katherine and Scott to the resort. He had volunteered to be her escort and help with the luggage. The hotel boasted over six hundred rooms of various sizes, each with its own accouterments. The suite reserved by Katherine was nearby to Nusa Dua beach. Guests of the resort could enjoy nature trails, swimming pools, shops, cafes, restaurants, fountains, exotic plants, and grocery stores; other requests were handled by the concierge. As Katherine found out, the only reason to go to the city was for a change of pace because the Hyatt had almost every desired amenity.

At the same time she and Scott went to the Hyatt, Ronnie and Joel taxied to Denpasar to see the sights. Mike elected to stay on the yacht. He wanted to call Jennifer. It was Friday noon in Bali, 3:00 p.m. in Sydney when he called her cell number. She was home early from work, showered, and was finishing toweling off. After their initial hellos, she answered his first question before he had a chance to ask it.

"I got the money, all ten thousand," she said. "It's in our savings account. You might get a dollar interest eventually."

"That's okay," he replied. "So long as it's in the bank."

"Are you in Malaysia?"

"We stopped in Bali," he remarked. "We're at the Royal Bali Yacht Club."

"Bali!" she exclaimed.

"It's on the way and we're ahead of schedule, so it made for a good stopover. Ronnie and Joel are excited; they already went to town."

"I'm jealous. We planned to go to Bali once, remember?" she said.

"I remember," he replied, hoping to avoid any other comment on the subject.

"Did you talk to Wilson's son?" she asked.

"Yeah. He was engaged to the woman that was killed. He was at the house, but he'd been knocked out."

"That's what someone else told me," she said.

"A guy workin' for his father killed her and the other guy. He had to get on the yacht or his mother would've been killed. I've no reason not to believe him."

"Can he identify the man who did the shooting?"

"I don't know. I didn't ask."

"Does he know his name?" she asked.

"Didn't ask him that, either," he remarked.

"So, how long will you be in Bali?" she inquired.

"A week. It'll take a week to get to Malacca from here. That's more than a week to spare and gives the boys time to see the sights."

"Just the boys?" she chided. "Mike, let me know if you learn anything else. And promise you'll call before you leave Bali. I'll call if I want more information from your passenger or just to talk. Between him and another person I met, I may have a good story. Is Scott Wilson there with you now?

"He went to check out one of the resorts …You doin' okay?" he asked.

"I'm okay. Is Bali as nice as they say?"

"I don't know. I haven't been off the yacht."

"Well, enjoy yourself, but be careful, Mike. Remember, steer a straight course. I miss you. I love you."

"Luv' ya', babe," he replied, with little emotion.

After checking in at the resort, Katherine and Scott walked to her suite where they relaxed in the living room, both opting for a soda from the mini-bar. While she unpacked her bags in the deluxe bedroom, he inspected the other bedroom, kitchen, and patio, and then they decided to stretch their legs and walk around the property. After strolling the area for a while and getting a bite to eat, they returned to her suite before going to the beach—close by, as advertised—and sat down in the shade of a date palm tree. A pleasant breeze moderated an afternoon temperature that had risen to 30°C.

"You picked a great place. It's got everything," he said.

"Well, it may be the only time I visit here, so I wanted something nice. It helped that I got a twenty percent discount through my office."

"You work in real estate, right?" he asked.

"For five years. I quit nursing. Can you imagine? Now I take care of properties instead of patients. The pay is much better than nursing, and at this time in my life financial security is more important to me than devotion to a nursing pledge."

"I suppose," said Scott, distractedly.

"Why do I get the feeling you don't agree? You must have joined CARE to help in their work without thinking about the financial rewards. Is that it?"

"Well, yes, but if truth be told I'm secure financially, so I'm able to do that …but you mentioned devotion to a pledge. Shouldn't the priority be devotion to the patient?"

"Of course. And so you don't think too terribly bad of me, you should know I keep up my credentials. I take continuing education courses every year."

"I guess I've been put in my place," he said.

"Do you mind if I ask about your girlfriend?" she asked. "Mike told me what happened to her."

"It was just over three weeks ago," he said, "but …sometimes it still feels like I'm waking up from a nightmare."

"What will you do when you go back?" she asked.

"The only reason I have to go back is because my mother's there. Shoot, I really need to call her."

"It's hot. You can call from my room," she advised.

"I tried a lounge chair in the lobby when you checked in. I'll call from there, then get a cab back to the yacht."

"Are you sure it's no problem?" she said.

"Using a phone in a crowded lobby can be surprisingly private if you're snug in a leather recliner," he said smiling.

"Okay. Be that way. If any of you want to join me for dinner, call me," she said walking toward her suite.

Scott found a recliner in the lobby and phoned his mother's residence. Sandra Morse answered.

"Hello, Sandra. Is mother home?"

"No, I'm sorry, Scott. She's in a meeting."

"When will she be back?"

"Soon I think. She's been gone two hours."

        Ronald Lutz

"Well, tell her I'm okay. I called and left her two voice messages. Hope she got them. Tell her not to worry."

"She is worried. Will you be stopping by?"

"I had to leave the country; I'm calling from Bali. I'll be here for another week and then on to Malaysia. So I'll be gone several more weeks."

"I'll make sure she knows. I've written it down. Bali for a week, then Malaysia, and back in a few weeks."

"Okay, thanks, Sandra," he said, concluding the call.

James Wilson was seated at the balcony table in the Grace Hotel suite, a cigarette dangling from his lips. Ray Dunn was mixing drinks in the kitchen and carried one to Wilson before returning to his seat on the couch with his own drink in hand. He was using the remote control to scroll through television channels when the doorbell sounded. He muted the TV and went to the door.

"It's Lindsay," he called back to Wilson.

"Okay," Wilson said, a permission for her to enter.

A young woman with long brown hair and wearing a charcoal gray skirt and white top came into the room. Without a word being spoken, she handed Wilson a manila envelope. He examined the contents, looked at her, and nodded his approval. She retraced her steps and left the room.

Wilson gave the envelope to Dunn. "There's two boarding passes on Virgin Air leaving tomorrow morning for Bali. Tell him to take a girl; he'll look more respectable."

"I'm not sure he knows any girls," Dunn said.

"You're kidding," responded Wilson. "Well ...Chelsea can go along. Don't tell her too much. Just to enjoy herself."

"It's a seven-hour flight, isn't it?" Dunn asked.

"With a three-hour time change," stated Wilson. "It should only take him a couple of days. The return ticket is for next Monday. He may even have time to go to the beach."

"You must a' seen Eddie Gilds to get a flight that quick."

"Yeah, but he couldn't pay for them," Wilson admitted. "I had to use my card."

"So that takes care of Denham," Dunn said.

"I still have to decide about the yacht," Wilson added.

"Foster said some kids were workin' as crew."

"They'll have to fend for themselves, same as my son."

"You gonna do anything about the reporter?" Dunn asked.

"She can't know anything or she wouldn't keep trying to call me," responded Wilson.

"Yeah, that's true," Dunn said. "She saw your ex after the cops were there. Sounds like she might be an ambulance chaser."

"She'll need an ambulance if she shows up at my place again." He smiled, leaned back and took a drag on the cigarette.

"Another contract," Dunn stated drolly.

"Something else could be worked out if it comes to that. Terminating her job with the paper, for instance." Wilson stated unsympathetically. "I'm not worried about her nosing around. Turns out she's married to the boat jockey; if she does cause trouble it wouldn't be a good idea to knock both her and her husband off, not that it wouldn't be out of the question. Besides, I've always enjoyed her opinion columns, even the ones she wrote to bad-mouth me. We'll respect our media for now; freedom of the press, you know. They've always been good to me. How 'bout another drink?"

CHAPTER EIGHTEEN

The morning of the second day in Bali the beach was unexpectedly unoccupied except for Katherine and Mike, sunning themselves after swimming and frolicking in the ocean; relaxing on complimentary hotel blankets, they were soaking up the sunshine. She wore an itsy, bitsy red bikini with a triangle top; Mike had on dark blue Joe Boxer trunks. The day was bright with an almost cloudless sky. Because it was 30°C they did not stay in the sun for more than a few minutes at a time but sought the shade of one of the cabanas, also provided by the hotel. The contrasting warm temperature and cool water definitely aroused their senses as did the use of a liberal amount of sunscreen applied one to the other.

"I see why people call this paradise," she said, stretching her lithe body onto a recliner, then continued, "We can go to Geger Beach sometime if you want." She pointed toward a distant beach. "It's just up there; I heard it's a nude beach."

"I suppose I could be your chaperon," he suggested.

"Have you ever been to one?" she purred.

"Yes, and I got sun in all the wrong places," he teased. "'Getting burned' took on a whole new meaning. Here's *my* idea. We could rent a Jeep and tour the island with Ronnie and Joel."

"That sounds like fun too. I guess there's more to Bali than the Hyatt, but so far it's living up to all my expectations."

"It's nice," he said.

"Are you and Scott ...I mean is it worth your while to go to Malaysia? I hope I'm not getting too personal."

"You are," he said stone-faced, then smiled, "It's worth it to me. I'll be able to finance my own boat. Scott's onboard cause his ole man wanted him outta town. He pays all the expenses but far as I know he's not gettin' anything."

"His father wanted him out of town?" she repeated.

"Never mind. I shouldn't have mentioned it."

"But you did," she stated. "Now you have to tell me."

He paused a moment. "A man was killed the same time as Scott's girlfriend. Scott wasn't involved, but he was in the house. His ole man's a politician and didn't want anyone to find out Scott was there 'cause he figur'd his chances to get reelected would go bye-bye, so he got him on the yacht."

She pulled her recliner into an upright position. "So Scott was a witness?"

"No, he was unconscious," Mike answered.

"But if he was there, he must know what happened."

"He's kept quiet; a threat was made against his mother."

"You're making this sound like an episode from *True Crime*. Did you know all this when you took the job?"

"No, but I suspected somethin' was up. I went along with it 'cause a' the money ...and the cruise. When we were on Boigu I called my wife. She filled me in on some of what's been goin' on. Scott told me some more on the way here."

Katherine readjusted her recliner, leaned back, and was momentarily silent, then spoke to Mike while gazing at the ocean.

"You've never mentioned your wife; I guess I never asked. It's been stupid of me. I took it for granted you weren't married. You don't wear a wedding ring."

"Never wore one. I've seen guys on boats lose a finger 'cause they wore a ring."

"How awful."

Several other beachgoers trampled over the sand near where they sat and occupied their attention for a minute.

"How long have you been married?" she asked.

 Ronald Lutz

"Ten years, but we knew each other in high school."

"A lifelong love. How nice," she said, sincerely.

"Not exactly. We were ...well, I joined the navy and she went to college. We went our separate ways, but met again later on," he remarked, summarizing their separate journeys.

"Do you have children?" she asked.

"No," he said, with more than a hint of remorse.

"Does she work?"

"She's a journalist, an investigative reporter for the *Daily Telegraph*; it's a Sydney newspaper."

"That's impressive.... I was married three years in my late twenties after I finished nursing school. It didn't work out; I guess I was too independent for him."

"You strike me that way. But you're easy to look at, so it fig'urs there's been lots a' interested fellas."

"Not so many as you might think," she said. "But a few."

They gazed at one another for a moment.

"How 'bout another swim," Mike suggested.

After their swim they had lunch, and then Mike returned to the yacht. It had been agreed Scott would get the afternoon away from the boat. Katherine used her time alone to enjoy a massage and later joined Mike and Scott for dinner in an Indian restaurant in Denpasar.

———

LOSING TRACK OF TIME IN BALI IS NOT ONLY EASY, IT'S ALMOST expected. The third morning Katherine and Scott lounged around a swimming pool. Having enjoyed her massage the previous day, she suggested they get a spa treatment. After they were all rubbed and scrubbed she called Mike. He had been doing maintenance work on the yacht, and she asked if he could join them at a cultural dinner show at a location near the resort. When he got there later he thanked them for giving him directions. Other similar dinners were in progress.

"I walked past at least three Polynesian luaus," he said. "They all seemed to be doing a good business."

He was wearing nylon convertible pants and a tropical print shirt. Scott wore the same clothes he had on all that day. He had washed and dried them in Katherine's suite. She had on a brown print, rayon dress with spaghetti straps adjusted to a low neckline with a hemline well above the knee.

Decorative landscape lights directed the diners to rows of tables on a lawn facing a darkened stage lit only by flaming torches. They took a seat and Polynesian music began to play as dancers with hand-held lights moved through the dining area. The four-course meal—appetizer, salad, a main course of roast pig and dessert—was to be accompanied by several musical performers, comedians, and a ritualistic interpretive dance.

"We've already had a couple of drinks," she told Mike.

"Then I've got some catching up to do," he remarked and ordered a beer from the waiter.

"I hope the roast pig tastes as good as it smells," she said.

"I don't feel like a Luau," Scott said, excusing himself. "I think I'll walk on the beach; maybe find a bar." Over their objections, he gulped the last of his drink and left the table.

"If I didn't know him better," Mike spoke out. "I'd say he was going on a prowl."

"I don't think so," she said.

"When I was his age I'd be lookin' for a nice Indonesian girl. Some of 'em can charm the socks off ya', an' more an' that, if you let 'em."

"The way you say that you must have known one or two."

"Sometimes it was hard to avoid, cruisin' 'round and all."

"Before you were married, no doubt?" she asked.

The waiter brought Mike's drink, and she changed the subject.

"What else besides piloting yachts interests you?"

"Being on the sea interests me," he said. "I been on one vessel or other most of my life. I helped my dad, then joined the navy, and

 Ronald Lutz

most recently operated tour boats." He smiled "I even served on a cruise line that disappeared."

"Disappeared ...oh, you're kidding," she exclaimed.

"It was run by a Chinese guy. He took his ships and went back to China, or parts unknown. Left his creditors high and dry. I was one of 'em."

"What did you do after that?"

"Signed on with Carnival Cruise Line. I was there a few years until they started extendin' their ports o' call. Worked mostly on charter boats since then."

"That's quite a resume," she said.

"I haven't got rich, but I pay my bills." He drank some of his beer. "The thing is, I love bein' on the sea and that makes the jobs I've had worthwhile. That's my story, what's yours?"

"I've told you. Hong Kong real estate. It has lots of ups and downs, kind of like the stock market."

"Lived in Hong Kong long?"

She smiled at his alliteration. "Almost all my life. Father brought mother and me from England when I was three. She died the next year. I grew up in his office; he was a GP, a general practitioner."

"When did you decide on real estate?"

"Not until later. Father sent me to Taipei Medical School, then to Hong Kong University for premed. I switched to their School of Nursing and after graduation worked at a private clinic until after he died. I liked it, but the money in real estate was too much of a temptation."

"Your resume's not bad, either," he said. "Ever think of goin' back to England, like when the Brits pulled out?"

"No, unless things change. Hong Kong is my home."

"Won't be going back to Boigu either, I'm bettin'."

"Well ...not for a while. I called Al yesterday. I wanted to tell him we made it okay."

Dinner interrupted their talk. They enjoyed the meal of roast pig and other delicacies. Afterward, while having a drink, Katherine removed a camera from her clutch purse.

"Care to see the pictures I took when we arrived?"

"Sure," he answered.

"It's not serious photography, but I have fun with it." Leaning over to hand him the camera she exposed more than ample cleavage and then purposely caressed his hand causing a faint blush to softly touch his cheek.

"Gently manipulate the joystick." She said suggestively, obviously referring to more than just the camera.

"Yeah, I see," he said, reluctantly happy.

She leaned in again, "I particularly like that one. You look very much like the captain of a yacht."

After viewing the pictures, Mike examined the camera. "Nokia. Don't think I've seen this model. It's a nice size."

"It's not just the size, it's what you do with it."

He returned the phone. She leaned back and crossed her legs seductively, briefly exposing all that could be exposed.

He paused, then continued, "I'd suggest another drink..."

"We could have it in my room," she interjected.

" ...but I'm expected back, the boys want to go to town."

"Those boys!" she responded. "I've been liking them until now. Well ...maybe we can have that drink later."

"Tomorrow," he suggested.

They walked to her room, and as he said goodbye, she pulled him to her and kissed him passionately on the lips.

"I'm sorry you can't stay. Thanks for a wonderful time."

"You invited me, remember." He returned her kiss.

"Couldn't you call the boys and tell them you're delayed?"

"They're expectin' me. I'll call you tomorrow."

"You know what they say, never put off till tomorrow ..." Not finishing the thought she kissed him again and went inside.

"See ya," he said, walking away, looking back at her suite.

 Ronald Lutz

CHAPTER NINETEEN

The night darkness further disguised a man in black as he watched Mike board the yacht, certain he was the man he looked for. He received a confirmation when Ronnie called Mike by name as he and Joel prepared to leave. After they had gone, Mike turned on the radio in the saloon and began cleaning up the bar. Wavelets from a passing boat splattered against the hull of the yacht and onto the pier lit only by halogen lamps, spaced far enough apart so that one could easily imagine ghostly images dancing in the dark. The man in black further darkened the pier by loosening two of the lamp bulbs closest to the yacht; he wore black latex gloves and had blackened his face. Inside the yacht, Mike finished cleaning, turned off the radio, and was on his way to the bedroom when another boat sped past. Feeling a slight shift of the tie-up ropes, he decided to check if the lines were still securely fastened to the cleats. The man on the pier had his hand on the toe rail about to come aboard but moved back in the dark when Mike came out and descended the gangway.

When Mike stepped onto the pier, the other man pulled a stiletto knife from a belt holster and lunged toward him with a stabbing motion aimed at the heart, but he slipped on the water that had splashed on the pier and missed his mark. Mike cried out in pain as the knife punctured his skin and skittered against the outside of his ribs, causing an entrance and exit wound from the one thrust. The attacker fell on top of Mike, and they both struggled to gain an advantage, but Mike was weakening from the loss of blood.

Returning from his beach walk, Scott heard a man cry out as he approached the yacht. He could hear scuffling on the pier and called out a loud shout even as the man with the knife was about to make another stab. Scott yelled loudly a second time, and the man in black dove into the water and swam away. Scott ran up to assist the victim and realized it was Mike.

"Mike! Are you okay?" Scott asked, then saw the blood.

"Get me on board," Mike said, holding his side.

In the saloon Scott immediately wrapped a sheet tightly around Mike's body, closing the wound on his side.

"That needs to be looked at. I'll call an ambulance," Scott said. "Do they have 911 on Bali?"

"You can try it," Mike said.

Just then Mike's cell rang. Startled, Scott answered even as he thought to disconnect so he could call for help.

"Oh, hello," Katherine responded. "You didn't waste any time getting back from the bars. Is Mike there?"

"Someone attacked him with a knife," Scott declared.

She was reclining on the bed and sat up at this news.

"How bad is it?" she questioned.

"Who is it?" Mike asked.

"Katherine," Scott mouthed. "Well, the bleeding seems to have stopped. He was stabbed along his side. I don't know if he needs to go to the hospital or not."

"I'll be alright," Mike said. "Tell her it's alright."

"You're sure the bleeding has stopped?" she asked.

"Yeah, looks like it," Scott said after a brief inspection.

"I'll be there in fifteen minutes." Throwing off her robe, she slipped into a paisley print tunic dress and sandals and grabbed a small treatment bag from her suitcase.

She paid the cab driver extra to get her to the pier as fast as possible and was on the yacht nine minutes later, arriving the same time as Ronnie and Joel returned from the city. Seeing the blood on the deck, they hurried onto the yacht and met Scott outside Mike's room. Katherine removed the sheet and examined the wound. She asked Ronnie to get clean warm water in a basin, Scott to find bandages, and Joel to assist her if needed. Then she washed her hands thoroughly.

"You didn't need to come here," Mike complained.

"This way you won't have any hospital bills," she said, returning to his bedside. "Besides, I specialize in house calls. Think of it as my way of repaying you for bringing me here."

Ronnie returned to the stateroom, and Katherine checked the ingredients of an ointment that was in her bag. By the time Scott returned with the bandages she had cleaned the entrance and exit wounds with a washcloth, applied a thin layer of ointment, numbed the area with an agent she also had in her bag, then closed each wound with several stitches, and dressed the wounds with bandages. She gave Mike pain pills before going to the washroom to clean up.

"You're as good as a nurse," Joel stated.

"She was a nurse, once upon a time," Mike said.

"Looks like a real professional job," Scott added. "I'm glad you called when you did."

"Change the dressing every day," she said, "especially if it gets wet or dirty. If the redness spreads or it doesn't seem to be healing there may be an infection. We don't want that to happen, so take care of it."

"Thanks," Mike said.

"Are you going to report what happened to the police?" Joel asked.

"No," Mike answered. "I don't know what he was after, but I bet he won't be around here again."

"We should tell them," Scott said. "Attacking someone with a knife is serious business."

Mike relented. "You're right. I'll report it tomorrow."

<hr>

October 30

THE NEXT MORNING MIKE WAS ENJOYING A GLASS OF ICED TEA while sunning himself on the top deck. Katherine came up the stairs from the lower deck. She had stayed overnight on the yacht and was wearing the same tunic from the day before. She visually examined him and inspected the bandage closely.

"Joel changed it a little while ago," he said.

"It's fine," she said. "Just remember to change it every day until it heals. And don't stay in the sun too long."

"Yes, Nurse Ratched."

"What did you say?"

"Just makin' fun," he said. "Nurse Ratched was a character in a movie I saw when I was a kid. What I meant to say was you're lookin' mighty sexy today."

"Thank you. But this is the same dress I wore last night."

"You're the sexy one, not the dress."

"Would you rather I take it off?" she offered.

He smiled at the suggestion. A pitcher of tea was on the table, so she gave him a refill and poured herself a glass before sitting and demurely crossing her legs.

After sipping the tea she began to stroke her crossed leg. "Don't you think my legs are one of my best assets?"

"I prefer your lustrous blue eyes," he said sincerely.

"You're certainly full of compliments today," she said. "Tell me, Mike, what's the color of your wife's eyes?"

He made a grimace and pursed his lips. She did too.

"That was bad of me, wasn't it?" she said. "But I've got an excuse; I was up half the night with a patient."

"I did thank you, didn't I?"

"Well," she remarked, "there's one way to say thank you, and then there's another. Anyway, thank Scott. He stopped the bleeding."

"I suppose you're goin' to hold me to what you said last night, about being repaid for bringing you here?" he kidded.

"I believe you said that would be fair."

He went on, "I must have been delirious. A few stitches and

 Ronald Lutz

that pays for everything?"

She smiled, "You can make fun all you want, but it could have been a lot worse. I guess I'm naïve, but I never once thought assault or street crime would be a problem here."

"Me either," he said.

"Did he try to rob you?" she asked.

Shaking his head no, "Seemed like he was hell-bent on killin' me. Could be he thought I was somebody else, or he wanted to burglarize the yacht and I got in his way."

"Did you get a look at him?"

"No. He was big, bigger than most men around here."

"Did you tell that to the police?" she said.

"I asked Scott to talk to them."

"Good idea. You should take it easy today. You'll be sore a few more days," she said, getting out of the chair. "Rest. Do as little as possible for the next day or two. I'm going back to the hotel and get cleaned up, but I'll call later and check to see how you're doing."

"Bye, beautiful," he said as she climbed down to the pier.

———

SHE DID CALL LATER. SATISFIED HE WAS BETTER, SHE DECIDED to go to an outdoor poolside theatre production. That evening while Mike rested, Ronnie cleaned up old bandages and other items from the night before and gathered up dirty laundry.

"There's a lot here to wash," Ronnie said, "but I'll do it tomorrow. Joel and I are going to the arcade in town. It was closed last night. Scott's onboard if you need anything."

Scott walked into the hall as Ronnie came out of the room.

"See ya," he told Scott. "Joel and I are going to town."

"How is he?" Scott asked.

"Don't ask; he exaggerates," Mike shouted from his room.

"You sound well enough," Scott said looking in at Mike as Ronnie climbed to the main deck carrying the laundry.

"I'm fine. You don't have to hang around," Mike said. "But get me a couple of beers before you go. I'm too lazy to climb the stairs, and Joel's on the pier waiting for Ronnie."

"We may be out of beer, but I'll check," Scott stated.

"Joel restocked it. I made sure of that," Mike boasted.

"Okay. Be right back," Scott said, smiling.

He went up to the main deck saloon toward the galley.

"Don't turn around," a voice commanded him.

"What ...?" Scott exclaimed as the man, dressed like the night before, pulled his arms behind him and secured his hands with plastic ties. "What are you doing here?"

"You remember me?"

"I remember," Scott said as a rag was stuffed in his mouth.

"You're lucky I saw you come up the stairs. Your ole man wouldn't have wanted me shootin' you by mistake. By the way, he said to tell you to have a good time. From the looks of that chick I saw you with at the Hyatt, you're doing okay."

He immobilized Scott by strapping him to a chair.

"Somebody yelled last night," he said. "If it was you blame yourself that I had to come back. This time I've got a gun, but everything will be real quiet."

As he started down the stairs, he offered Scott a consolation.

"Your crew boys will untie you after I'm gone."

He descended the stairs to the lower deck and checked the master stateroom before going to the open door of Mike's stateroom. As he peered into the room, Mike looked up.

"Got a gun this time, Denham."

He raised his gun to shoot but a "chick-chock" sound caused him to whirl around. He fired a bullet at the same time the shotgun pellets struck his body. He fell to the floor dead. A bullet grazed Ronnie's arm; he dropped the shotgun in pain.

Mike: "The skin's torn. Get something to stop the bleeding ...How does it feel?"

Ronnie: "It burns."

Mike: "You saved my life."

Joel: "I heard the shots. Is he dead?"

Mike: "Yes."

Ronnie: "He tied up Scott."

Mike: "Hold that tight."

Ronnie: "Can we call Katherine?"

Mike: "We need the police. Where's Scott; is he okay?"

Joel: "He's tied up in the saloon."

Ronnie: "It's still burning."

Mike: "Okay, I'll call her. Joel untie Scott; tell him to get the police."

Mike: "Keep pressure on it, Ronnie...Katherine?"

Katherine: "Hi. Missed me, huh?"

Mike: "I didn't want to bother you..."

Katherine: "Are you alright?"

Mike: "Ronnie's been shot."

Katherine: "Is this a joke? What's going on over there; did your side open up?"

Mike: "It's no joke. He was shot in the arm."

Katherine: "I don't believe it; is it bleeding?"

Mike: "No. I think he'll be okay."

Katherine: "Make sure you've stopped the bleeding; elevate the arm and keep pressure on it. I'll be there as soon as I can."

Mike: "She's coming. Elevate your arm; keep pressure on it."

Scott: "Is he okay?"

Mike: "Yeah. Call the police, will ya'?"

Scott: "He's the guy that killed my fiancée."

Mike: "He would have killed me if not for Ronnie."

Scott: "He ran by me with the shotgun. All I could do was hold my breath. Maybe we should call Katherine."

Mike: "She's on the way."

Ronnie: "I'm thirsty. Is there something to drink?"

Joel: "I'll get some water."

> Earlier, as Ronnie carried the laundry from the lower deck to the main deck he saw, in the mirrored wall of the saloon, the intruder holding a gun. He hurried on to the utility room and grabbed one of the shotguns. Loading two shells, he then retraced his steps through the saloon and down to the lower deck in time to confront the gunman.

Katherine arrived wearing a tropical print shirtdress she wore at the poolside play. She was shocked to see the dead man. Mike was talking to the police, so she checked Ronnie and applied the same first aid to his arm as she had the night before for Mike. After the police removed the body, they were conducting interviews and Katherine found herself in Mike's room. She was looking in her medical bag for some pain pills when Mike walked in.

"I've got pain medicine in here somewhere for you and Ronnie," she said.

"I don't need any, Katherine," Mike stated.

"Oh sure," she said, close to tears. "Why use painkillers? In the past day you've been beaten, knifed, and almost shot. It's amazing your wound didn't open up again tonight."

"I have you to thank for that."

"Well," she said, trying to smile. "If this isn't the end. We're alone in here and all I can do is play nursemaid."

He took her in his arms and kissed her on the lips. She gently pushed away and looked at him to see if he was serious.

"Maybe you're right," she said. "You might not need painkillers," and she returned his kiss passionately.

He locked the door. Immediately they were overpowered by sexual arousal. He lifted her in an embrace and they started to disrobe while moving toward the bed. At that moment Scott knocked on the door and asked for Katherine.

"Yes?" she asked, impatiently.

"Ronnie's got a problem," Scott answered.

"What is it?" she asked, clutching her dress.

"The wrapping came loose and he says the pain is worse."

"If it was anyone else ...," she said under her breath and then so Scott could hear. "I'll be right there."

Dressing quickly, she reached the door but Mike caught her arm and turned her to him. They kissed again. Scott was waiting outside the room when she came out.

"Are there any more bandages?" she asked.

"I think so," replied Scott.

"Aspirin, ibuprofen?"

"I don't know," he said.

"Ask Joel. There must be an apothecary somewhere."

"I'll check my briefcase," he remarked. "I may have some travel packets."

Scott went to his stateroom across the hall and took hold of his bag and searched in an outer pocket. He pulled out several small aspirin packets along with a digital disc in a paper sleeve. He stared at the disc, forgetting for a moment the aspirin in his hand.

CHAPTER TWENTY

— October 31 —

The next morning Mike sat on the outdoor lounge aft and Scott stood close by. They had watched the DVD the night before and, at Scott's urging, Mike had just called Jennifer.

"She wants to see it," reported Mike.

"That's all she said?" asked Scott. "She wants to see it?"

"She seemed to be more concerned about the attacks," Mike added. "She was troubled Ronnie had been hurt."

"I thought she was a reporter," Scott stated with more than a little agitation. "Elections are less than three weeks away."

"She thinks yours is the only remaining copy."

"That's what I figured. I thought I heard Scarface say the rest were destroyed. There's not much time," he complained.

"She'll call back; she's good at her job."

"I can't believe I had it all this time," Scott said sadly.

"How do ya' think it got there?" Mike asked.

"Harriet must have put it in the briefcase after we watched it, so it's been in the bag all the time. Apparently, the guy smashed up the wrong disc."

What did happen? When Ray turned away from her to look at Scott, Harriet noticed the messenger bag close to her at the foot of the bed and resolved at that moment not to give up the DVD without knowing Ray's intentions. She slid the DVD into the exterior pocket and picked up the CD disc

                    Ronald Lutz

from the bed; it was in a similar paper sleeve. She held it out to Ray when he turned back to face her just before the gunman shot him. After shooting her, the gunman broke up the wrong disc.

"Do you think Jen can get it published?" Mike asked.

"She should get it distributed to all outlets plus Instagram, Twitter, Facebook. It'll blow father's campaign sky high."

"Ya' gotta be careful," Mike suggested, "'specially when ya' think ya' got a sure thing."

"Well, what they say on the video can't be more clear."

"Who they are matters as much as what they say," Mike said. "I recognized the PM. The other guy is your father?"

"Yes. He owns this yacht."

"Can't say I've ever seen him," Mike added. "But then I don't follow politics all that much."

"Trust me, he's a big shot," Scott added.

"I'm sure Jen knows who he is," Mike offered.

"He says in his own words he was involved in illegal deals and unethical contracts," Scott stated. "And you can't deny he was out to get you. There's no mistaking what he said, but I didn't remember you as being the Mike Denham in the video until last night." He paused, "I'm thirsty, I'll get us some drinks."

Katherine came aboard and met Scott in the galley. He directed her to Mike on the main deck lounge.

"Ahoy there, skipper." Mike smiled at her greeting.

She walked onto the deck wearing a nautical blue and white shirt dress, looking remarkably cool considering it was already quite warm.

"Mornin'," he replied and got up to help her with a chair, touching as much of her body as discretion allowed.

"I see you're a morning person," she said.

"You bring out the sailor in me," he remarked as they sat down, "you and that perfume you're wearing."

"Would you say it's intoxicating?"

"Well ..."

"It's called Intoxication, designed to put you under my spell. How's Ronnie?"

"Sleeping. Whatever you gave him knocked him out."

"Good, I was hoping for that." She readjusted the deck chair. "Sorry I couldn't stay last night. I was exhausted."

Scott returned with drinks.

"Hello again," she said to Scott.

"Can I offer you a drink: beer, wine, scotch, bourbon, vodka, gin?" He smiled broadly and handed Mike an iced tea.

Katherine smiled too. "You're in a good mood. I'll take whatever you gave Mike, as long as it's nonalcoholic."

"One more Joel's iced tea coming right up," he said, turning to go back through the saloon to the galley.

"How's your side?" she asked Mike.

"No pain, no redness, feels good."

"Excellent. Then you can join me at the beach later. We can have dinner and watch the lawn movie they're showing at the resort, if you're up to it."

"Any room in there for a little romance?"

"We'll make room." They gazed at each other warmly.

Scott returned with the tea. "Here you go, Katherine."

"Thanks," she said appreciatively.

"Mike looks pretty comfortable sitting there, don't you think?" Scott asked her.

"Comfortable, yes, but not all that pretty," she kidded.

"When the police finish, I'll be good to go," Mike said.

"Where to?" Scott asked.

"Malaysia. A buyer's expectin' delivery of this yacht in a couple a' weeks. Remember?"

"Maybe," Scott said. "But if father tried to kill you here, it might mean you weren't even supposed to go to Malacca. Don't forget what he said on the video."

"A friend of mine got me this job. I can't see him bein' involved in something like what you're describin.'"

"Father can make his schemes seem very innocent. He may have told your friend only what was needed to hire you."

"Your father had something to do with what happened here?" Katherine asked.

"Yes. He hired Mike to transport illegal immigrants ..."

"To test a ship," interjected Mike. "They loaded it with illegals."

Scott went on " ...when he reported the illegals to immigration, my father found out and put Mike on a hit list."

"A hit list!" she said. "More *True Crime*."

"My father's a major political figure in Australia," Scott answered. "I found a video of our PM and him talking about illegal activities they've been engaged in while in office. They talked about the immigration report Mike filed too. We watched it last night after you went back to the resort."

"So what are you going to do?" she asked.

"Distribute it to the media," Scott answered. "It's a matter of informing people. What's on it will expose them for who they are and show the voters they shouldn't be reelected. With all they've done, they should be in jail. And it's not just political wrongdoing, father crippled my mother years ago and had my fiancée murdered because he didn't like her looks."

"I take it back," she said. "This is better than *True Crime*."

She looked from Scott to Mike and back to Scott.

Scott explained, "He's always been able to protect himself by the power of his position in government; he hides behind a wall of yes-men. The video exposes some of the corruption that guides his life."

Mike interrupted, "Before you go on, I'd like to find out for sure about Malaysia." To Scott, "Can you get the number for our Malacca contact? It's in the dresser in my room."

"Sure," Scott said and he went below to get the number.

"Did you know all that he said?" she asked Mike.

"I don't follow politics, but I have to say it's convincing for a five-minute video. You'll see it."

Katherine approached Mike and checked and adjusted his bandage. "I didn't know what to think when you told me his fiancée had been killed," she stated. "Now there's this other thing about his mother."

"Altogether it points to more than corruption," he said.

"I wonder what happened that his mother was crippled?"

"Father tripped her," Scott said, returning. "I know because I saw him do it; I was thirteen. He caused her to fall down a staircase in our home; she's been paralyzed ever since. I told her what happened but no one else listened to me. After a year of therapy she divorced him anyway on other grounds."

"Did she get a settlement?" Katherine asked.

"No, she only wanted out of the marriage," Scott said, and then asked Mike, "Is it the same time in Malaysia as here?"

Mike nodded in the affirmative. Scott tried to call the number on the buyer sheet three times and always got a "no such number" response. Then he tried a person-to-person call to Malacca and was told there was "no such name or address."

"That confirms it," Scott said. "Our trip was a setup."

"To get you out of Sydney," Mike stated.

"But you were obviously a target," Scott said. "The Malaysia trip was a scam; some kind of phony plan."

"An elusive getaway?" Mike suggested, then declared, "Didn't you say the guy who tried to kill me was the same guy who killed your fiancée."

"That's right," Scott answered.

"Well if that's so, he had to come from Sydney. How'd he know I was here? We'd only been here three days when he first jumped me."

"I ...don't know," Scott said.

"The only person I talked to was my wife," Mike stated.

"I called Al," Katherine said.

"I tried to call my mother; she wasn't home," Scott said.

 Ronald Lutz

"Ronnie and Joel called home from Boigu, but that was before they knew we were coming here," stated Mike. They didn't call again till last night after Ronnie was shot."

"Now that I think of it, I talked to one of mother's caregivers," Scott recalled. "But that's all."

———

UNLIKE THEIR PREVIOUS TIME ON THE BEACH, NUSA DUA WAS crowded when Mike met Katherine later that day. Rather than frolic on the sand before dinner, they stayed in her room and resumed their passionate foreplay from the night before; the sexual interplay led to intercourse. Much later they called room service for a light meal and champagne, then skipped the outdoor movie and continued making love that evening, finally falling asleep in each other's arms after midnight.

Sunlight caused shifting shadows to filter through the curtains of the suite the next day. Katherine was asleep on the bed next to Mike. He'd been up attending to his wound, and when he returned to rest in bed he thought of different things, *She's passionate and beautiful; Ronnie saved my life, had he fired that shotgun before? The police should finish their investigation soon; I wonder if Wilson had planned this all along; Sleeping there she looks so calm, so content; I want to hear what Foster knows.* Then he fell asleep again and had a very visual dream. *{His father turned to look at Jennifer and him seated in the stern of the boat. From the ship's wheel, he smiled at them showing pearly, white teeth and said, 'We'll be home before the sun sets.'}*

Mike awoke with a jolt because of the realistic vision of his wife and deceased father. It roused Katherine from her sleep, and she looked at him drowsily.

"Hi," she murmured.

"Good afternoon," he replied.

"Afternoon?" She exhibited no inhibitions, rolling off her stomach and exposing her naked body.

"I hear some women don't look as good in the mornin' as they did the night before. No one could say that about you."

"You're sweet. You know, I was dreaming about you."

"Oh."

"Yes, you were going away somewhere," and she began to cover herself with the sheet.

"To the yacht? I should go to the yacht," he said.

"Are you really that anxious to leave?" she asked.

"I've ordered breakfast," he declared.

"You were very quiet; I didn't hear a thing."

"I used the phone in the bathroom," he said. "I hope you like fried rice with tomatoes, a poached egg, fried bananas, coffee, and orange juice. Oh yeah, and I got a bowl of fruit."

"I just realized I'm famished. And you ...you must be psychic; I would have asked for the same thing."

"I know. I found an old order card you filled out."

She smiled and allowed the sheet to fall away again. "How much time do we have before the food gets here?"

A knock on the door and room service was announced. They both first looked surprised, then she pretended to pout. Mike smiled broadly and put on a robe and went to the door. He invited the server to enter the suite as she slid back under the sheet; sunlight streamed into the room.

"Is it really afternoon?" she asked.

———

It was late afternoon when Mike returned to the yacht from the resort. Scott was on board.

"Looks like the police have decided our story is on the up and up. They've found a woman who was with Malone."

"Malone?"

"Well, yeah, the guy Ronnie killed," Scott explained. "He was hard to identify. The police said he didn't have anything on him. No phone, keys, key card or wallet; nothing."

"How did they find out?" Mike asked.

   Ronald Lutz

Scott, slightly annoyed at being interrupted, continued.

"Because when he tied me up, the guy said he saw me at the Hyatt. When I told the police about it, they took his photo to the main desk and asked if they'd seen him. Turned out one of their surveillance cameras took his picture with a woman that had registered as a guest and the police tracked her down. They don't think she was involved. She said they were here on a holiday and had return tickets to Australia. They weren't married."

"I'd say that's damn good police work."

"Yeah. Once they found her, they ran a trace to see if they could get more information about the guy."

"How is Ronnie; is he here?"

"He's doing okay," Scott said. "He and Joel went into town. I tried calling Malacca again. Got the same response."

"You might be right about a phony buyer," Mike said. "I'll try one more time tomorrow. If I can't connect, we'll have to figure out what to do."

"Have you called your wife again?" Scott asked.

"I've left three messages," Mike answered. "When we talked the other day she said it might be a couple days before she got back to me. If I don't hear from her by tomorrow, I'll call her office."

"Well, I'm thinking I might catch a flight home," Scott said. "Even if she calls, it may be the only way to get the video distributed. Problem is, I don't know who to go to."

"What about the police?" asked Mike.

"I'd rather try another media outlet," Scott suggested.

"You're right, that may be better," Mike agreed.

"I'll have to check on some flight schedules," Scott said.

"I'm meeting Katherine for dinner," Mike stated. "You're invited too. She asked me to tell you to come."

"What time?"

"I'll leave around seven," replied Mike

"I'll try to make it, but I want to run some errands, so if I'm not back, don't wait for me," Scott answered.

CHAPTER TWENTY-ONE

Neap tide signaled a fast-approaching dusk and Scott had not yet returned to the yacht. Ronnie and Joel had agreed to stay on board so that Mike could meet Katherine; he did not wait for Scott and got to her room as she was getting in the shower. She asked him to get an outdoor table at a nearby restaurant while she finished dressing. About the time he had been served a second drink the hostess walked by him to show another customer to a table, but the person ignored the hostess and stopped behind Mike and placed her hands over his eyes. He tenderly took the hands away from his face and began to kiss the palms thinking it was Katherine but then saw the wedding ring. He turned to see *Jennie!*

"Hi," she said, and then kissed him on the lips, obviously glad to see him. He was astonished to see her.

"I thought I'd surprise you," she added. "But you kissed my hands like you were expecting me." She placed a camera and briefcase on the table before sitting down. She wore a maroon cotton top with three-quarter cuffed sleeves, slim white ankle jeans, and maroon converse high tops. Mike was speechless.

"What's the matter, cat got your tongue?" Jennifer teased.

Regaining his composure, he spoke with a hint of sarcasm. "No, it's just I was expectin' a call."

"Isn't this better?"

"What're you doin' here; how'd you find me?"

"I'm here to see how you are. The last time we talked you said you were at the Royal Bali Yacht Club. I found the yacht, but Joel said I just missed you and that you were here. He also said you

     Ronald Lutz

were hurt more than what you told me, which is what I figured. You have a way of minimizing things. Remember your appendicitis? So I left my luggage on the yacht and used the spy app on my phone to track you here. Pretty good, huh? You look good. Are you okay; what exactly happened?"

"It was a knife attack, like I told you."

"Joel said you were stabbed. That's more than what you said on the phone. It certainly doesn't happen every day."

Katherine, wearing a pink strapless dress hemmed above the knee and blue open-toed sandals with ankle straps, had approached the table but her gait slowed when she saw the blonde woman.

"Excuse me. Am I interrupting?" she asked.

Mike stood up. "Jennifer, this is Katherine Decker. Katherine, my wife." Jennifer was immediately disquieted by the attractive appearance of Katherine. Katherine thought Jennifer appeared very chic in her sporty attire.

Mike called the waitress and they ordered drinks. Not sure what to say, the two women looked at Mike.

"Katherine is stayin' at this resort," he said.

"Have I upset your plans?" Jennifer asked.

"It doesn't matter," Katherine stated. "We were going to have dinner. Mike didn't say *you* would be here."

"Well, I like to surprise him, but the older we get the less fun it is, especially after he's survived two attacks on his life."

"It was rather frightening," Katherine stated.

"Were you there when it happened?" Jennifer asked.

"I've had some nursing training and helped with the cleanup. He's probably glad he brought me here from Boigu."

"You're from Boigu?" Jennifer asked Katherine.

"Hong Kong. I was visiting my brother there. Bali was my next destination, and Mike agreed to bring me."

"So you had time to get acquainted?" Jennifer reasoned.

Mike, increasingly uncomfortable, asked for some menus.

Katherine went on, "I understand you're a reporter."

"Yes, for the Sydney *Daily Telegraph*. Mike called and said there might be a story for me here. When I learned he'd been attacked, I took time off to find out what happened."

At her last remark, Mike turned an appreciative look toward her that did not go unnoticed by Katherine.

"Can we go inside?" she asked. "I've suddenly developed a chill." It was 27°C.

Dinner was over when Scott joined Mike, Katherine, and the attractive blonde.

"I thought you'd be outside," he said to Mike.

"I'm surprised you found us," stated Katherine. "You could have called."

"That was my next option," he said, sitting down. "How was your meal?"

"I recommend the chicken breast," Katherine suggested.

"I'll just have a drink. I grabbed something in town."

The waiter came and they ordered more drinks.

"Scott," Mike cut in, "This is my wife, Jennifer."

"I thought so. Mike's tried to call you," he remarked.

"I had my phone on airplane mode on the flight," she said.

"You came from Sydney?" Scott questioned.

"Yes."

"So you're here to see the video?" Scott asked.

Jennifer nodded yes. "And I was concerned about Mike."

"Oh, sure," Scott said. "It could have been a lot worse."

"Were you injured?" Jennifer asked.

"No. I was tied up, that's all."

"A bullet grazed Ronnie's arm," Mike added. "He was hurt as much as anyone."

"I saw he had a wrapping on it," Jennifer stated. "It must have been a traumatic experience for everyone."

"It wasn't pleasant, that's for sure," said Scott.

"What I'm going to ask may be equally unpleasant," Jennifer began, turning to Scott. "Do you know anything about the deaths of Raymond Dowling and Harriet White?"

"They were murdered. My father was responsible, but I don't know how to prove it," Scott stated.

"Did you witness what happened?"

"No. I'd been knocked out. When I woke up they were both dead. But Malone was there."

"Malone?"

"The man who murdered them," Scott said. "The guy Ronnie killed after he attacked Mike."

"The man that committed the murders in Sydney was here in Bali?" she exclaimed.

"Yes. I'm sure my father was behind it. I was knocked out. I think he didn't want the media to find out I was in her home," Scott said. "He believed his campaign would be hurt, so he got me on the yacht by threatening my mother's life and he used the yacht voyage as an excuse to try and murder Mike."

"So you're saying your father hired the man that killed Harriet and Ray, and he was also sent here to attack Mike."

"Yes."

"Do you know why he had them killed?"

"No. I wish someone would explain it to me."

"You might be interested to know there's another witness who supports some of what you're saying."

"Who?" Scott questioned.

"He hasn't revealed his name, but I think he worked for the Brown campaign. Based on what you've said, you can probably understand why he's wanted to remain anonymous."

"Well sure, but I don't get it. Was he in the house?"

"He says he watched from an open door on the deck and saw Raymond Dowling being murdered and was there for much of everything else until you left."

"What else was there to see?" Scott wondered.

"It's not so much what he saw, but what he heard. The gunman mentioned your father and the fire at the annex."

"Some things are hard to remember," Scott said. "I thought other copies of the DVD might still be out there."

"None have turned up. Presumably, the annex at Brown headquarters was burned to destroy all the copies. By the way, did you call for an ambulance to go to Harriet's home?"

"Yes. I didn't want her body lying there on the floor. Malone let me call from his car."

"So Mike said you have a video. Can I see it?"

"Sure, and I had some copies made in town. That's why I got here late. I was going to send you a copy." He handed her the DVD. "It's yours to keep."

"I have a DVD player in my room," Katherine announced, and under her breath, "Maybe I'll get to see it that way."

"If we do that, let's take some drinks," Mike suggested.

He called a waitress and they ordered more beverages.

"If you can use the video," Scott said to Jennifer, "please remember my mother has been threatened. The video can't be linked to me in any way if she's to remain safe."

"We can do that. Do you have any other family members we need to know about?"

"No. There's only my mother."

"I talked with her last week. She was worried; she hadn't heard from you. Have you called her?"

"I've tried. So far I've only been able to leave messages."

A drink cart came to their table. Katherine signed the bill, but Jennifer promised she would be reimbursed.

"My room is next to the statue of Venus," Katherine stated.

     Ronald Lutz

CHAPTER TWENTY-TWO

— November 1 —

A video had been discovered incriminating two major politicians, one a possible conspirator in a murder. It was blockbuster news. But the enthusiasm and resolve Jennifer needed to further investigate the story was missing, and it wasn't because her husband had survived two attacks. It was because of his apparent involvement with Katherine.

She didn't need to see a marriage counselor to know that Mike was attracted to Katherine and vice versa. They had been together for two weeks. Was it an infatuation? Had they made a commitment? Probably not. Had they been to bed together? A ladies' man before they had wed, Mike had never been with another woman during their marriage as far as she knew ...until now? If he and Katherine were considering a relationship, they would have to decide their next step. All she could do was remind Mike she loved him.

Sitting on a chair in the master stateroom, Jennifer watched Mike apply shaving cream and begin to shave. He had on khaki shorts; she wore a sleeveless, V-neck tropical dress.

"Scott will be flying back tomorrow," she remarked.

"You too?" he asked from the bathroom.

"What are your plans?" she asked.

"Go back to Sydney. Malaysia was a hoax."

"Are you going on the yacht?"

"That's what I figured. Don't want to leave it here."

"Then what?" she asked.

"I'll find something; I always have."

"And what about me?"

He stopped shaving and looked at her in the mirror. "You'll be with the paper, right?"

"Yes," she said, looking back at him, "at least for a while."

"Well, then," he stated, and finished his shave.

"What would you say to my going back with you?"

"That'd take a while. Can you miss that much work?"

"How long would it take?" she asked.

"Two weeks or more," he answered.

She shook her head. "I don't think it matters ..."

He splashed water on his face and dried himself with a towel.

"What about your story?"

"Dennis can handle it."

"Look," he said with resignation, "I know you're involved with a guy. You don't have to play any games about wanting to go back on the yacht. It's alright. Go with Scott."

"I'm not involved with a guy! Why would you say that?"

"I saw it on your computer," he said.

"What!" she exclaimed. "Show me. Here's my laptop."

"You don't have to do this, Jen. Go back to Sydney."

"I want to know what you saw."

"Go - back - to - Sydney."

"What - did - you - see?"

He looked at her. "On your computer at home ...a letter."

"Our computer," she corrected him.

"You're the only one who ever uses it."

"So you saw a letter; what letter?"

"To David."

Recent visits to Haggerty made it easy for her to remember.

"You must have read a draft of an email. Something I wrote when we were separated."

"It wasn't that long ago. I just saw it last month."

"But it was an old letter. You saw a letter I deleted from the computer, not long ago. It was a draft of a letter that I had sitting in a 'hold' folder I never mailed."

"Come on, Jen. You wrote a letter and didn't send it?"

"I have lots of documents in that folder. Documents I keep to review or wait to take action on later or for whatever."

"How many other letters to this guy are you holding?"

"None. But you should know when we were separated I did have a brief affair with him. I never told you because at the time I thought we were going to be divorced. After we got back together it didn't seem relevant."

He sat on the bed. She sat down next to him. "Can you forgive me for something that happened a long time ago?"

"Forgiveness isn't one of my strong suits."

"I know. I hope you'll try. Please try. We're together now, and that's what counts. Please try to forgive me."

Scott knocked on the door. "Everybody decent in there?"

"Come on in," invited Mike.

"Thought you two might join me for lunch," Scott said.

<hr>

November 2

Wednesday morning in Bali and another day in paradise. At least it should have been. Katherine and Mike were on the lower aft deck of the yacht outside the master stateroom. She was wearing the rayon dress she wore earlier in the week, and he had on shorts and a sport shirt.

"I thought it was an evening flight," she remarked.

"It was moved up."

"Is that why she isn't going?"

"We decided ...she thinks it'll be fun to go back on the yacht, like when you came here."

"It was fun; it was an adventure. But I was also very attracted to the captain.... Why did she go to the airport?"

"Last minute instructions. She wrote down everything and wanted to go over it again with Scott. Our elections are two weeks from tomorrow; he's got a lot to do in a short time."

"What about us; will our time together be short too?"

Mike looked at her thoughtfully but said nothing.

"My former husband gave me the silent treatment too."

"You've got a lot going for you," he said. "Beauty, talent, you're smart. You can't go wrong with that combination."

"He never said I was smart," she said, brushing off a tear.

"He wasn't payin' attention. It's one of your best traits."

"So what are Jennifer's traits?"

"I'd rather not talk about her."

"Oh, come on," she prodded. "It can't be that difficult."

"Well, she's no wallflower; no shrinking violet."

"So I noticed. What else?"

"If you want to know, she can be arrogant, demanding, and stubborn."

"Do you love her?" she asked

He looked at her, and then looked away.

"I thought we were in love," she said.

"I'm sorry," he said. "It wasn't going to work. You're going back to Hong Kong, and I'm going to Sydney."

"Thank you for telling me to my face," she said, brushing away another tear. "But you know it could have worked. We could have made it work."

She stood up, turned on her heels and went inside.

RIDING WITH SCOTT IN AN AIRPORT TAXI, JENNIFER WAS SORTing through the papers filed in her tote. She was wearing a gray, cashmere wrap over a white top, pull-on twill pants, and white block-heel sandals. She had twirled her hair into a high, tight fish-tailed bun. Scott sat slumped beside her and pretended to look at the countryside, all the while wondering if going back would open

     Ronald Lutz

up wounds that had not quite healed. He had paid to get a makeover above the neck and was unrecognizable to anyone who might know him. He had on the same outfit he wore when he first boarded the yacht almost a month before, but now he had black hair and sported a thick black, well-trimmed fake beard with mustache and wore tortoiseshell colored Sinar Maju glasses. At the airport, clutching his carry-on bag and with no luggage to check, he confirmed his ticket, got his boarding pass, and then sat down next to Jennifer in a public area and waited to enter the security line to the departure gates when his flight number was announced.

"I'd feel a lot better if you were going with me," he said.

"I would too," she noted. "But right now I need to be with my husband." She handed him a paper. "Here's a checklist. You know what to do. It's a reminder more than anything."

"A grocery list," he remarked.

She pointed to the paper. "At the bottom are my email addresses. And the satellite phone numbers. Did you get the dish in Denpasar?"

"At a marine supply. It's got a WorldView antenna. You'll be able to phone, fax, watch TV, whatever," he replied.

"Was it expensive?"

"Very. At least, with Mike setting it up, we avoided the installation costs."

"He's good at those types of things, but I noticed he had you and the boys helping out," she said.

"We tested it. There should be no communication problems on the ocean."

"If we leave tomorrow we may get back in time to vote."

He looked at the list again. "So first I contact your anonymous source."

"That's the number at the top. What do you think? Is he Terry Godfrey."

"It might be," he stated. "Your description of him wasn't a lot to go by."

"Between the cap pulled down on his head and sunglasses it was hard to know what he looked like," she remarked, "but I doubt his disguise is as good as yours. You're like Blackbeard with glasses. Who did it?"

"Hair Bali," he answered.

"Really? I saw one of their ads at the resort," she said.

"Well, when I go through security I'll find out how they like my new look. It's sure not like my passport photo."

"I didn't think of that," she remarked.

"It shouldn't be a problem," he said. "So after I contact Terry, or whoever it is, we go to the paper?"

"Right."

"What if he won't go?"

"You'll have to convince him. Make sure he knows the gunman is dead. It shouldn't be any harder than convincing him to use fiber optics in your father's den."

"If he talked about that, it's gotta be Terry. So then we go to the paper and I'm his assistant, or co-worker or something."

"Whatever's believable."

"And we see you're colleague at the paper."

"Dennis Williams. I circled his name and number in red."

"He'll know we're coming?"

"Yes. I mailed him a disc Air Express and included a letter explaining who you are. He should have it when you get there but take one of your copies just in case. And make sure your contact emphasizes the DVD was taken from the annex before it burned. Tell them he found it later in his luggage, like you did. That's so my bosses know the reason it's been a month since its discovery."

"Yeah, that's good. That should protect my mother too. Who are your bosses?"

"Jason Cosgrove is the managing editor. Dennis will introduce you to him. I'm sure on this type of story he'll want you to see Anita Varisok, the executive editor, and our vice president, Charles Gordon. Of course, they'll want to watch the video and probably

          Ronald Lutz

interview both of you."

"You think there'll be any problems?"

"Something usually comes up. Someone from the paper will try to contact Wilson or his press office for a comment, but after that the story will be set in motion and everything will be made ready as an exclusive for our paper. Our parent company, NewsCorp, will coordinate a distribution release with Foxtel, their broadcast partner."

He kissed her on the cheek. "What was that?" she said.

"Sorry, I got carried away. Distributing the video is such a big deal, but I know there'll be more to do."

"Right. No matter what happens at the paper, go see David Haggerty at the city center police station. I've called him and explained the situation. He's expecting you to contact him, and I'm sure he'll want to interview you and my witness."

"David ...?"

"Haggerty, his name is on the list." She underlined his name. "What you've got on the video is politically explosive; it could lead to criminal charges; conspiracy to commit murder is another possible charge. Haggerty will want to hear your story and the story of my other witness."

"Have you worked with him before?"

She paused briefly. "Yes. When I talked to him last time he said the Indonesian authorities had already been in contact with our Foreign Affairs office about Malone. They may be able to link him in some way to your father."

"That was quick."

"The other thing: you wondered about the woman that works for your mother. Haggerty agreed to get a tower dump to see if she used her cell phone to call your father. They'll get the landline data too. If she called him, we'll find out."

Just then a public address system announced Scott's flight.

"Are you sure you can get through security?" she asked.

"Yeah. If they give me a hard time, I'll tell them I had a small part in one of those 'Hangover' movies they shot in Denpasar last week."

He walked into the security line and then turned back to look at her. "I forgot to tell you something," he called out.

'What?' she mouthed.

He mouthed back 'Ask Mike' as he entered the line.

———

WHEN JENNIFER RETURNED TO THE YACHT SHE FOUND KATHerine lounging on a chair on the main deck outside the saloon.

"Mike's in the galley making sandwiches," she said.

"Oh," replied Jennifer. "I'll go ask him to make one more."

"Don't bother. You can have mine; I'm not hungry."

Jennifer put down her briefcase and removed her wrap, trying to think of what to say as she sat down.

"Scott get off alright?" asked Katherine.

"Yes, he's on the way."

"I was surprised you didn't go with him."

"There's really nothing more I could do," said Jennifer.

"Mike said you'd be writing the story for your paper."

"Well, my staff will help out, but since they installed the satellite dish, I can write some of it on the yacht and email it.... How much longer will you be here?" Jennifer asked.

"Another week," Katherine stated.

"That sounds wonderful. Mike and I were going to visit here several years ago but never got around to it."

"If you're not needed for the story you should stay."

"Mike notified customs he wants to leave tomorrow," Jennifer stated. "With Scott gone, we can't pay for any more extra days."

"I've been with Mike, Scott, Ronnie, and Joel a lot," Katherine said. "I guess I'll have to make some new friends."

"Too bad you weren't able to get someone to come with you, or did you prefer to come alone?" Jennifer asked.

"It didn't work out," Katherine replied. "No one wanted to go with me to Boigu. A friend of mine would have met me here, but she canceled when I was in Boigu."

"Well, I doubt you'll have trouble making new friends. You seem to me to have an outgoing personality."

"Sometimes. It depends on who I'm talking to. You're easy to talk to. Is that because you're a reporter; I suppose it helps to be outgoing as a reporter?" Katherine inquired.

"I'm an extrovert by nature, but if anything I think I've become more reserved since I've been a reporter.... I was told you work in real estate?" Jennifer asked.

"I manage about six hundred units for a Hong Kong firm."

"That must keep you busy."

"Most of the time. Something's usually going on.... I like your outfit. It would be a good look in Hong Kong."

"Thanks." She looked at the label on the wrap. "I bought it in Sydney. It's lightweight, but right now I'd rather be wearing your dress. Is it rayon?"

"Yes, and I think I'll wear it out on this vacation, I'm in it so much. I may get something else at the Hyatt shops. So far my only purchase is a perfume I bought in Denpasar."

Mike came out on deck with a tray of sandwiches and a beverage container. He stumbled when he saw Jennifer, but regained his balance.

"Careful, sailor," Katherine said. "You've been here a week. You can't still have sea legs."

He smiled a wry smile. Jennifer got up to help him, taking the beverage container and a glass.

"You should have kept your stewards on board to help, Captain," Katherine suggested, with a wry smile of her own.

"Oh, shut up," he said politely. "Here's some sandwiches."

"I'll get another glass."

"I'll get it," said Jennifer. "I want to change into something cooler anyway."

She retired into the master stateroom to change clothes.

Katherine looked at Mike. "So you're leaving tomorrow."

CHAPTER TWENTY-THREE

Scott arrived in Sydney late Wednesday night, and after checking into an airport hotel, he called his mother. This time she answered. He made a sincere apology for not contacting her sooner and went on to explain what was going on. Saying he would visit her soon, he asked her for the time being not to let anyone know he was back in Sydney, especially Sandra.

After talking to his mother, he called the number for the anonymous witness and asked for a prompt return call, giving his name and cell number and explaining he had received the number from Jennifer. He waited four hours, until almost midnight, for Terry to call. He was happy to learn Terry was the other witness. Terry was relieved to know the gunman was dead and elated to learn the video had been salvaged. They agreed to meet in the hotel room, and Scott remembered to tell him he had a makeover. It was 1:00 a.m. by the time Terry arrived at the hotel. He arrived and instantly remarked about the makeover, but right away they began to go over their plan of action: to visit the newspaper and meet with Haggerty. After a while, they stopped to catch up on the election race.

"Our poll numbers haven't changed much at all," Terry said. "We ran new ads, but your old man keeps hitting Brown with false negatives."

"I saw a couple on TV," Scott remarked. "Maybe we can change that after we visit the paper. How soon can you go?"

"Whenever. Just let me know. I'll pick you up."

By the time they met again later that morning, Scott had purchased new clothes at an airport men's store. He had also called

 Ronald Lutz

Dennis Williams to make sure they were expected at the *Daily Telegraph*. Terry drove them to the newspaper office. It didn't take long to satisfy the executives that the recording was authentic. After they reviewed the video, the three executives began to set in motion the story for the paper just as Jennifer had predicted. Media affiliates were contacted and told to prepare for a nationwide release; a television news broadcast was scheduled for the next day. Before going to the police, Terry called Leonard Brown to advise him of the day's event.

⸻

November 3

KATHERINE SAT ON THE BEACH UNDER THE SHADE OF A DATE palm tree. It was almost noon and already 32°C. She wore Persol sunglasses and was dressed in white capri pants and a sheer pink top, and carried a wide-brimmed sun hat. A white silk scarf with a Hong Kong logo served as a belt. Mike was scheduled to depart midday on the return voyage to Sydney and would motor toward the east. She waited to see if the yacht would be visible. Clearly upset, she removed a small green tin box from her pocket just as a sun-tanned man wearing a slim fit bathing suit stopped in front of her, briefly blocking her view. He was close to her age, short of stature, huskily built with more hair on his chest than on his head, but he had a pleasant face. One hand was protected by an elastic bandage.

"I hope you won't mind my saying," he said, "you're very sensibly protected from the sun."

She looked over her glasses at him showing an uncaring smile.

He went on, "I usually take precautions to shield myself, but didn't even use sunscreen this morning."

She nodded, this time with a 'don't bother me' smile.

"If you like, I can get one of the cabanas for you."

"Thank you, but I'm only going to be here a few minutes," she said, curtly.

"Well, enjoy," he said, making a half turn to go, adding, "You might see a cruise ship out there. I've seen them from here, and I saw a yacht from Geger beach a while ago."

"I thought about going over there," she said. "Is it nice?"

"Not any nicer than this beach."

She mentioned, "I heard you can go topless."

"And bottomless; it's a nude beach. So I guess if you're there and can't spot any yachts there are other things you can look at," he said, smiling cautiously.

Katherine grinned, "Did someone catch you looking?" she asked, removing her sunglasses and pointing to his bandage.

He laughed, "No, I was fooling around playing cricket.

"I've never really understood that game," she said.

"It's just bowl ball, bat bowl, and know a few rules."

"Are you playing here?" she asked.

"I don't play competitively anymore; I'm an honorary captain. We were in Australia and stopped here for R & R."

"Where's home?" she asked.

He spun sideways and pointed to a Hong Kong logo on his bathing suit. At that, she showed him the logo on her scarf.

"A souvenir or do you live there?" he asked.

"I've lived there most of my life. So do you take time off to travel or are you independently wealthy?"

Laughing, "I'm a stockbroker for Boom. They graciously allowed me to accompany the team this time. You?"

"I work with Hong Kong Association; real estate."

"I live in one of their properties, by Head Road," he said.

"I know it. That's a nice one," she said warm-heartedly.

"Are you staying at this resort?" he asked.

"Yes."

"I wonder, would you like to get together for a drink later? If you're with someone, bring them along." His smile showed even white teeth.

"I don't know. Can I call you later?"

     Ronald Lutz

"This is my room number." He drew his room number in the sand. "If we agree on a place, it'll be my treat."

As he started to leave, she called out, "What's your name?"

He turned back toward her. "Mark ...Mark Dayton."

"I'm Katherine."

He had a pleasant smile and could, after all, explain to her the rules of cricket. Pocketing the green tin, she turned away and failed to glimpse *Getaway* motoring east, but paused to verify the number in the sand before walking off the beach.

AFTER THEIR MEETING AT THE *DAILY TELEGRAPH*, SCOTT AND Terry went to the city center police station and waited almost an hour for Haggerty to return to his office. He came back with a box of doughnuts and handed them to the receptionist. She said the men were waiting, and he invited them into his office.

"I've been expecting you," he said. "The *Daily Telegraph* reporter contacted me and said you'd be here."

"We were at the *Daily Telegraph* earlier," Scott offered. "We showed them the video. They're going to distribute it."

"Do you have another copy?" Haggerty inquired. "If so, I may want to watch it with you."

Scott said, "I've got one."

"When is it going into distribution?" Haggerty asked.

"They said it would be on TV tomorrow," Scott replied.

"And now you're here because of what happened at Marrickville," he said knowingly.

"Right. It's been reported Ray Dowling killed Harriet, but that's not the way it happened," Scott said.

"Which one of you is Scott Wilson?" Haggerty asked.

Haggerty checked both their identifications, remarking how little the documents Scott provided looked like him.

"I got a makeover in Bali," Scott explained. "I hoped it would help keep my mother safe. She could be in danger because of the video. She was threatened last month."

"Who made the threat?" Haggerty asked.

"My father," responded Scott.

"Is James Wilson your father?" Haggerty asked Scott.

"In name only," answered Scott.

"I understand from Mrs. Denham you both have accounts of what happened at Marrickville." Haggerty turned to Terry, "And you're the witness to what happened there?"

"Yeah, I was on the back deck."

"That was a month ago. Why haven't you come to us before now?" asked Haggerty.

"I was scared," he responded. "I still am, but I found out the guy that killed Ray and Harriet is dead."

"Well, I'd like a separate deposition from each of you. We can get you together later if needed."

Their statements did not provide enough direct evidence to charge Wilson with a crime.

"Why don't we look at your video," Haggerty suggested.

"Sure." Scott handed him his copy.

"Is it an exact copy of what was originally recorded?"

"Yes."

"We can watch it in our screening room," Haggerty said. The three of them were joined by two other officers. After the review, an investigative unit assigned to Haggerty reported the airline tickets to Bali were purchased by Wilson, furnishing a link to Malone. With the statements of Terry and Scott, plus the video and the new information about the tickets, the police had enough evidence to authorize a search of Wilson's home.

The search enabled them to charge Wilson with several counts of both civil and criminal conspiracy. Indictments to commit murder along with the other charges were filed. With the indictments and other media stories, any hopes for the upcoming reelection of James Wilson were derailed. He was duly charged in criminal court and released on bail pending a first court date. Within a week of

     Ronald Lutz

the November elections, Leonard Brown of the Liberal Party had overtaken Wilson and became the presumptive nominee for the Senate seat for New South Wales.

CHAPTER TWENTY-FOUR

— November 10 —

It was mid-morning, eight days into the return voyage of *Getaway* to Sydney. The yacht ploughed on through calm waters under sunny skies, and the ocean sea remained smooth as they neared the Great Barrier Reef. Joel was at the helm in the pilothouse, and Ronnie was asleep on the bench behind him. Mike and Jennifer were in bed together in the master stateroom. Previously engaged in lovemaking, they had been silent for the last ten minutes.

"Are you awake?" she asked quietly.

"No," he whispered.

"Did I tell you Scott kissed me at the airport?"

"Tryin' to make me jealous?"

"I was going to check my email from him, and I guess that's why I remembered it. I'll be right back."

"You're checkin' that more here than when you're home."

"But when I'm in bed, I'm all yours," she said.

"You and the laptop," he remarked.

"Alright, no email ...yet."

He looked at her out of the corner of his eye. He had showed little outward emotion when she told him of her affair, and he was no longer angry and disappointed about the email. She told him why she wrote it (she was in a vulnerable state of mind), why it was in her 'hold' file (she thought about sending it but decided to wait), and convinced him it was an old draft she had purged (it had been in the computer for years until she decided to delete old documents one day). In the end, he believed her account of the affair, that it had happened when they separated and she felt alone and insecure. Because his own indiscretion was in his mind it was easier to forgive her. But should he tell her about Katherine? He was about to speak when she reached over him for a small bottle by the bed.

"I bought this in Denpasar," she said. "It's a perfume called Intoxication."

"I don't like it," he said, not wanting to resurrect the image of Katherine.

"Silly, I haven't tried it yet."

He choked out a response, "I mean I'd rather smell your natural body odor than some phony fragrance."

"Katherine recommended it. I have to say, she was very nice; very attractive. Didn't you think so? And the way she fixed you and Ronnie up, she could have been a nurse."

"She had medical training before going into real estate."

"Do you miss not having her around?" she asked.

"Hadn't thought about it. But I agree with you that she fixed Ronnie and me up real good."

"Well, she's probably returned to Hong Kong now," she said, replacing the bottle by the bed. "I suppose we'll never see her again. But then you'll think of her when you feel that scar," she said, running her hand gently across his side.

"Not while you're around," and he grunted as though she were hurting him, then pulled her to his side.

"I'm happy to hear that," she said, snuggling against him.

They were enjoying each other's company in silence until Jennifer again broke the quiet.

"Scott said that after the police heard the testimonies and watched the video they got a warrant to search Wilson's home. They gathered enough evidence to charge him with conspiracy to commit murder."

"Did you think they'd be able to do that?" he asked. "I mean, Scott was unconscious most of the time, and you said the other witness couldn't identify Malone. If Wilson is as sharp as you say, he should be able to get around that."

"Keep in mind they had the video—in his own words. Once they got the warrant, they came across some things that were very interesting. For instance, Wilson had the original video in his safe."

"Why would he hang on to somethin' like that?"

"Who knows. Maybe he put it there and forgot he had it. But something he should have remembered was the licenses for the guns Malone used. They were in his safe too. One was for the gun he used to shoot Scott's fiancée and the other one for the gun he used to shoot Ronnie," she explained.

"That was considerate of him; keeping them around."

"Yes, wasn't it?" she exclaimed. "But what the police found that made it easy for them to authorize a search was the credit card information he used to purchase airline tickets for Malone and his girlfriend."

"You'd think he'd have known that could be traced."

"It was probably convenient for him. Obviously, he didn't think the attack would turn out the way it did. And aren't we happy about that?" she said, cuddling up to him again.

"I must have hit his wallet hard for him to send Malone all the way to Bali after me," Mike offered.

"Scott said it's just that he's a vindictive person."

"He must have quite an organization. Someone with the Sydney harbor master had to tell him I was going to go to immigration about the men I picked up in Brisbane."

"Well, wait to you hear this. Scott said a woman employed by his mother is the one who told Wilson you were in Bali. He thinks she told him about the video too."

"How'd they find out about her?"

"Scott figured she was the only one who could know you were in Bali and would have told Wilson. The police did a data dump of her phone records and confirmed his suspicion."

"They can do that?" he asked.

"With a court order," she responded.

     Ronald Lutz

"Wonder why she would be a tipster?" he queried. She started to explain, "According to Dennis …"

"How's he workin' out since his marriage an' all," he interrupted. "Don't hear you talkin' 'bout him that much."

"He's been great." She winked, "After you, he's my number one guy. Anyway, according to him, the woman's husband is a judge on a state commission. He had a kickback scheme of his own. Wilson found out about it and threatened to expose him, then offered to keep quiet if he got a percentage of the kickback. But when he found out the judge's wife was working for Scott's mother, he convinced him to get her to be an informer by threatening harm to her and their child."

"Why spy on Scott's mother?" Mike asked.

"He wanted to get someone in her home to find out what she and Scott were doing. Wilson knew they supported Leonard Brown and that she was hosting campaign events. It's just another example of how long Wilson's reach had become."

"How's the country supposed to survive with all this corruption going on?" he asked.

"Well, we've uncovered two of them. Maybe that will start some changes."

"What about the prime minister?"

"He's in for it too. Not for the murders, but for his involvement in some of the other scandals."

In fact, as a result of the distribution of the tape recording, Prime Minister Barnes lost his re-election bid to another Labor party candidate. His complicity in the corruption embraced by James Wilson led to a ten-year incarceration sentence and public disgrace. Released after five years from prison he retired on a social assistance pension and lived in a home owned by his brother in the state of Victoria. Wilson was sentenced to twenty-five years for conspiracy to commit murder. He died sixteen years later of lung cancer while still serving out his prison sentence. Their crimes touched the lives of several other people.

Wilson's campaign manager, Francis Offerman, had to rewrite a book he was able to publish called "Campaign Corruption". His original title, "Campaign Communicators", was changed along with significant content. He was hired by Australia's Nine Network as a political analyst and eventually moved to the United States to work for Atlanta's CNN International Bureau.

Ray Dunn slipped into obscurity. With no known ties to Wilson he moved to Melbourne and lived with his partner for several years before purportedly returning to Sweden.

Bernie Carlson was not so fortunate. He could not find employment with another political operative due to his association with Wilson, but appeared briefly on several television and radio talk broadcasts describing his involvement with the Wilson campaign. When those events ended he was forced to look for work elsewhere and ultimately found employment as a clerk in a retail store originally founded by Danforth Farrow. Unable to maintain his previous lifestyle, his home was repossessed because of failure to keep up with his mortgage payments and his wife divorced him. She was awarded custody of the children before marrying another press secretary who worked in her father's Senate office. Alcohol and drug use became an increasing problem for Bernie and he died from a cocaine overdose a few years later.

Some people's lives were changed in other ways. Terry Godfrey returned to work with the Brown campaign but after a year he and Shepherd Rayburn took positions with Telstra, an Australian company with an iconic brand name, and worked in high pay positions in their cybersecurity division. However, David Haggerty's position and work with the police continued in a routine way. He earned several more promotions and fifteen years later was promoted to the high rank of Deputy Commissioner. He and Susan were content, one could say happily married, throughout his years of service and she continued to teach at the pre-school in Parramatta.

Meanwhile, in the present day, the Leonard Brown donors all enjoyed a victory dinner at the Farrow estate with the presumptive Senate elect candidate. After all the attendees departed the estate, Margaret, in a somber mood thinking of the events of the past few weeks, retired to her bedroom, helped by her new assistant Janet Ogden. Sandra Morse had been dismissed, but in a spirit of forgiveness Margaret made no effort to file charges of invasion of privacy. Sandra's husband was implicated by Wilson and under indictment for his own corruption schemes. After getting in bed, Margaret opened her Bible to a passage in Hebrews: Hebrews 8:12 'For I will forgive their wickedness and will remember their sins no more'. Her thoughts centered on the potential of her former husband gone to waste; how his initial charm and enthusiasm in their relationship had turned to greed and corruption. Several years later she traveled to Bathurst Correctional Center on one occasion to see him and share some Bible passages with him, including the passage in Hebrews, and about her belief in God's love and forgiveness through His son Jesus Christ. He died without her knowing if the visit had any influence on the rest of his life.

Jennifer and Mike were quiet until she posed a question: "What about the money you were to get?" she asked.

"Let's put it this way, the contract he gave me wasn't worth the paper it was printed on. He probably figured he'd get back the ten thousand bonus too."

"What will you do with it?" she asked.

"I had something in mind if you can't use it."

"It's your money," she said.

"I might add it to what I've already saved and make a down payment on a boat."

"Will that be enough?"

"I'll double it if a guy I know matches me. We talked about going together on a charter operation."

"What guy?"

"Scott. It'll be a backup for his day job," he stated.

"That would be great if it's what you both want."

"Owning my own boat? I don't know why not."

"That must be what he was going to tell me," she said. "At the airport, he said he had something to tell me but I forgot about it till now. It must have been your partnership."

"And what about *our* partnership?" he asked.

"I pray it will be long and healthy," she said, sincerely.

She went to the bathroom and in a short while came out of the shower and walked toward the bed toweling herself off.

"You have a fantastic body," he said. The semblance of a smile formed at the corner of her mouth as he continued, "definitely a work of art."

"Is mine as nice as Katherine's?" she asked.

They made eye contact and stared at one another.

She continued, "You know, your big crush. Catherine, the Duchess of Cambridge: Kate Middleton."

He blinked and coaxed a smile. "Well, hers is nice, too, I suppose," he remarked.

"I think," she said, putting her hands on her abdomen, "I've been gaining weight. Here, put your hand next to mine."

She placed his hand on her belly.

He looked at her closely. "You couldn't prove it by me."

     Ronald Lutz

Then, noticing her slightly rounded form, he looked at her, and as they made eye contact again he understood what she was saying.

Smiling broadly, her heart was filled with joy because she could tell her husband she had finally been able to conceive. He gently stroked her abdomen and all of a sudden she started to laugh her robust, feminine laugh. Mike burst into laughter too. He had been bitter after reading the email but believed her explanation. He had forgiven her, understanding why she could have been unfaithful during their separation. Now more than ever he knew he loved Jennifer much more than he loved being on the sea.